Seeing

Audrey Wick

Cover Art by *Nicola Martinez*
White Rose Publishing, a division of Pelican Ventures, LLC
www.pelicanbookgroup.com PO Box 1738 *Aztec, NM * 87410
White Rose Publishing Circle and Rosebud logo is a trademark of Pelican Ventures, LLC

Publishing History
First White Rose Edition, 2023
Paperback Edition ISBN 978-1-5223-0422-7
Electronic Edition ISBN 978-1-5223-0413-5
Published in the United States of America

Dedication

To Yvette, a generous friend with a giving spirit.

What People are Saying

Past Praise for Audrey Wick

- Featured in the Family Fiction Summer Reading Guide

- Featured in Writer's Digest as a "Breaking In" profile

- Featured in Southern Writers Magazine as a "New Voice in Town" profile

- A Contemporarily Ever After Top Pick of the Week at Frolic

Past Praise for Island Charm

"Who doesn't love a beach romance? Especially when it's delivered in a way that is both entertaining and well crafted. Wick has a way of creating characters who stay with you long after you read the last page. Island Charm is perfect for an arm-chair traveler longing for romance and a suntan without leaving the comfort of home." —Beth Wiseman, HarperCollins Christian Fiction bestselling author

"Wick creates an enchanting world of mellow island charm as a lovely backdrop for effortless, breezy romance." —Susan Sands, Tule Publishing author of the Alabama series

"Likeable characters in a charming setting make this story the perfect little escape. I could almost taste the key lime pie." —Beth Carpenter, Harlequin Heartwarming author of the Northern Lights series

ONE

Hundreds of sets of eyes seemed to be staring at Danica Lara as she stepped into the waiting room of Spectacle Optique, Seguin's new eyewear apparel shop and optometry office. Rows upon rows of eyeglasses passed judgment from displays that surrounded the waiting room.

But she didn't want a shred of attention. Not any more than she had already received from her coworkers after mistaking the salt for sugar during her morning coffee routine. Or the jab from her best friend, Paige, when she'd sworn a quarter on the floor was her lost hinged hoop earring. Yet today, Danica felt like all eyes were on her anyway.

She hoped she wouldn't have to wait long for her appointment. She didn't know how much longer she could stand the staring.

Or her own vision.

She tugged nervously at her earlobe. The silver pair of drop lever-backs that dangled from them had not been not her first choice this morning, but at least she could find them both. Seeing clearly wasn't her strong suit as of late.

So at age thirty-two, she had made her first optometry appointment.

A too-perky receptionist greeted Danica as enthusiastically as if she were visiting her longtime hairstylist instead of an unfamiliar eye doctor. "We are so pleased to see you."

Danica choked back a laugh at the irony of the greeting. She slid her identification and debit card toward the attendant.

"Dr. Urban will be with you in a moment. While you wait, feel free to look around."

Danica signed her name on the digital check-in screen and wondered how many more puns the office staff had practiced. She wasn't sure how much word play she could stand.

"He's very proud of the new shop," the receptionist said.

Simple ergonomic chairs and accent pieces in crisp white coloring spoke to their newness. Indeed, the environment was much more chic than Danica had expected. Not that she expected much. She just knew her vision hadn't been the same in the past few months, and she'd bitten back her pride to schedule an appointment and find out why.

It wasn't that she couldn't see at all. She saw plenty of things perfectly: the clock on the wall that ticked by too slowly for eight-hour workdays, her wardrobe that could use an update, her singlehood status. It was just the little things she couldn't see, like words on a printed page or her computer's keyboard. She would have to adjust her distance in order to see straight, but even that practice wasn't predictable anymore.

So here she was.

She chose to sit next to a tasteful end table that held a few magazines as well as the latest copy of the town's *Gazette*. Track lighting overhead softened the space between the gleaming wood floors, exposed brick walls, and high-beamed ceiling. Oblong mirrors in delicate frames interspersed between the displays of eyewear made the interior seem bigger than it was, which magnified how small Danica felt.

She tugged again at the lobe of her ear and tried to shake the feeling of being watched by those rows of frames. To distract herself, she dug into her large leather handbag for a package of almonds that were her go-to snack—and, today, the main entrée of her to-go lunch. Popping almonds with one hand, she reached for the newspaper with the other before snapping it open on her lap to pass the time.

Five minutes and one *Gazette* police report later, her name was called by a second employee whom Danica followed into the examination room hallway. The blonde, who looked to be several years younger than Danica, introduced herself as Iris. "Like the flower." She smiled, prim yet peculiar.

Danica nodded a greeting, thinking an eye comparison would have been much more apt.

"Right this way." Iris led her around a corner.

Danica followed her until she felt the blunt force of something completely immovable hit her forehead. Wincing in pain, she squeezed her eyes shut.

And then everything went black.

~*~

Dr. Grady Urban was still learning how to schedule effectively. At times, an appointment went smooth as butter. Timing was exactly as expected, and he could stay on track client to client to minimize wait time. However, some clients demanded more hand-holding than others.

Poppy McDougal was one such client. She looked like she had walked off the set of a stereotypical southern chic-flick with mile-high hair and all manner of cosmetics applied thick as plaster. In spite of her waxy lipstick, her mouth smacked when she spoke her southern drawl, and whenever she leaned close to Grady, his nostrils filled with the sickening scent of musky perfume that smelled like it had expired—or been part of Mrs. McDougal's beauty routine for the better part of the century.

"And if you look right here"—Poppy grabbed Grady's hand—"you'll see that this part of my eye is bigger than this part over here. Now tell me why that is."

Grady had finished her routine examination, and he hadn't noticed any abnormalities. "What part, exactly?"

"Right here," she insisted, anchoring the skin beneath one eye with two fingers and pulling downward as if drawing open a window shade. "See?"

I don't. But Grady forced his most thoughtful face as he pretended to consider. "From your transfer records, your vision hasn't changed in the ten years since your cataract was removed."

"But, you see, honey, that's the problem." Poppy released her fingers as she sat back in the examination chair, the skin not as quick to slide back into place as the rest of her body. "That's why I came to you. Because you're new, and I think you might find something about me that my other doctor has missed."

"Oh?"

"Yes, you're fresh out of school and smart, and I can tell you take good care of people." Grady had to smile at that since he was trying hard to balance patient demands with office responsibilities. Optometry school, shadowing other professionals, and a formal internship had taught him what he needed to know about the profession, but he still felt woefully unprepared by the business side of Spectacle Optique. He had picked a desirable location in the Texas hill country, just thirty miles east of San Antonio. Seguin had deep-rooted history, pecan-tree-lined streets, and a quaint downtown. But establishing himself was harder than choosing a pretty location.

Three months into this professional venture, every new day still felt like he was posing as the owner of someone else's business. Although, the debt of his office's start-up was confirmation that this reality was his own. He needed all the patients he could get.

And he was learning to handle them with patience, too.

"Thank you," Grady offered.

Poppy winked at him, her lashes so full of thick mascara that they nearly stuck together in the same manner as her lips. "You are such a good-looking doctor. Handsome as they come. And strapping like mahogany wood."

Grady nearly choked as he swallowed the bizarre compliment. Uncomfortable flattery from a woman old enough to be his grandmother wasn't exactly his idea of an ego stroke, but he was learning how to adjust to the personality types of people of all ages in Seguin.

Poppy tapped her ring finger as she shook her head. "How you're not married is a mystery to me. Maybe if you get out of this dark room once in a while, you'll find a good Texas woman who just might—"

A loud noise from the hallway stopped Poppy and caused Grady to whip his head in that direction. A cry of "Dr. Urban!" rang in the wake of desperation that continued outside the patient room. A shocking cacophony of voices and moans and apology accosted him when he opened the door to the scene.

"What happened?" he asked.

Iris was kneeling by a woman who writhed on the floor clutching her forehead. Contents of the patient's purse splayed across the floor.

"She bumped her head, Dr. Urban." Iris implored the woman to let her see as she kept her hands in place and twisted out of her view.

And even though he had a sense, he asked anyway. "What did you hit?"

"The wall!" Iris and the woman screamed in unison.

That wall. Grady's own head shared agony at the situation. He'd known that load-bearing brick column was trouble from the minute the architect insisted it had to be kept in the renovation. Rounding the corner from the waiting room, he had worried it was too much in the way. But that's what he got with an old building. The quirks, he was told, added charm.

Now, looking at the woman who rolled to her side still clutching her head, he was ready to wrap that column in bubble wrap and have a firmer word with the architect. "I'm so sorry. What can I get you?"

The woman moaned as Grady bent to help her to her feet. At least his newest patient wasn't unconscious. "What do you need?" Grady offered the question to both.

"I think Danica is going to need an ice pack." Iris answered for the woman.

"Right," Grady said, completely out of his element. He dealt with eyes, not head trauma. "I'll get you something after I help you." He extended one hand and lifted under Danica's arm to raise her into a sitting position before addressing her in his gentlest voice. "How does that feel?"

She squinted at him through her one unshielded eye. "Peachy," she deadpanned.

At least she had a sense of humor.

"Iris, can you help her into the examination room? I'll get something cool for her head."

"Sure thing."

Grady made sure Danica was steady on her feet with Iris before they proceeded.

"Are we done here?" Poppy yelled through the din.

Samantha, the receptionist, appeared from around the corner. "Follow me, Mrs. McDougal. I'll get you all settled out here."

"Don't settle me like that one," she quipped, as if all three of them were directly responsible for the hit Danica took. "And what are these?" She froze in step to consider the spackling of tiny oblong objects that remained on the floor from Danica's spilled purse. "Did this woman lose her marbles or what?"

"We'll clean that up in a moment." Samantha urged Poppy on. "Just step right this way."

"I'll twist my ankle if I'm not careful."

"Take it easy." Samantha kicked a few of the objects out of the way. "They're just almonds."

Poppy's hand went to her chest. "I have a death allergy to peanuts, you know." Her face blanched. "And you didn't even ask me about that on any of the paperwork." She stepped through the mess with her nose high in the air.

"We're sorry about all of this, Mrs. McDougal. Let me offer you something complimentary to make up for the inconvenience."

Mrs. McDougal straightened and walked ahead. "Well, I could use a new notepad to use for my grocery list ..."

"Quite a *spectacle* I've caused, eh doc?" Danica's duplicitous question lightened the mood in spite of Grady's shock and professional embarrassment.

"I'll say."

"Have a seat here, Miss Lara." Iris gestured to a chair in an open exam room. "I want to check your pulse. Then we'll attend to your head."

"Let me find a cold compress. Be right back." Grady jetted around the corner to the only spot where cold items were kept. The breakroom mini fridge held a few beverages and the employees' sack lunches. He hadn't even stocked the tiny freezer space with ice trays.

Grady swung open the refrigerator door, seeing only one thing that would work.

Bingo.

He raced back to the examination room where Iris was assessing their optometry-client-turned-head-injury patient. "Have you ever had a concussion?"

"You mean before today?" Danica rubbed the side of her forehead.

This was far worse than Grady thought. "Do you really think you have a concussion?" His own mind raced with anxiety and fear for his new patient. Then there were more far-reaching issues, like the potential for a lawsuit.

"I have no idea." Danica squeezed her eyes shut.

"I just want to know what I'm dealing with." Grady's words were as gentle as his care.

"A patient who lost her marbles. According to that one." Danica kept her eyes closed but nodded in the direction of the doorway, as if to give a final jab to Mrs. McDougal.

"That one," Iris conceded, her voice lowered as if she were sharing a secret, "might just make us lose ours, too."

Grady stepped closer to Danica.

She opened her eyes.

"Maybe something cool will help your head?" He guided Danica's hand in a tradeoff for what was in his as he cupped his hand around hers so she didn't slacken her grip until the object made contact with her forehead.

"Mercy," she winced before sucking in a breath. "That's cold."

"That," Grady insisted, "will help with the swelling."

Iris cut Grady a look.

If her widened eyes could talk, they would have asked, "Are you kidding me?"

"It's all we had," Grady mouth backed with a shrug.

"I don't even want to see myself." Danica squeezed her eyes shut tighter as Iris placed two fingers on her exposed wrist to check her pulse.

"Heart rate is right at one hundred," she assessed. "Probably a little high for you. Let's get you calm."

"I think," Danica started, her words labored, "I passed that mile marker at the last turn."

Grady smiled at her continued quips, although he could sense her lethargy. And that part worried him. It worried him as much as his own uncertainty about his ability to sustain a new business, replete with accidents, surprises, potential lawsuits, and all. "We'll take care of you," he tried to assure Danica as much for her sake as his own.

She removed the cold object from her head, opened her eyes, and held it at arm's length. Her face contorted. "And so you're starting with this?"

He'd wondered how long it would take her to question his choice of a makeshift cold pack. And now he had his answer: less than two minutes.

"Is this a frozen yogurt pop?"

"It's really all we had." He forced a sheepish shrug. He could see the lawsuit details outlining right before his eyes. Patient hits head. Patient gets frostbite from a frozen yogurt pop. Patient sues Spectacle Optique for a million dollars.

"*Hmph.*" Danica turned over the pop.

"I think it's Greek yogurt. High in protein. And protein helps a body heal after trauma."

"Trauma?" Danica raised an eyebrow.

"Well, I assume that fall was traumatic for you." Even though he didn't want to give her any ideas, he wanted to acknowledge the accident just the same.

"This whole visit has been traumatic. Did you know I've never been to an optometrist before today?"

Grady hadn't gotten that far with her. "No. I didn't know that."

She tapped a finger atop the yogurt pop. "First visit. And I make a total fool of myself."

"Now, now," Iris soothed. "That's not true at all. We feel so bad about all this—"

"That your visit is going to be complimentary." Grady lunged at the offer to do something for her— anything at this point. "And we'll even throw in the yogurt." It was Iris's afternoon snack, but he'd worry about that later. His young assistant technician was much easier to please than a client who might just hit him with a negligence legal suit bigger than the state of Texas.

TWO

Danica wished the questions would quit coming. "Miss Lara, are you dizzy? Faint? Nauseous?"

Kind of hungry. For yogurt, actually. But Danica knew that answer would make her sound irrational. "I'm fine. Really."

Now that the shock of the· fall had worn off, embarrassment trumped her emotions. A small lump was forming at the corner of her forehead, though it was going to be annoying rather than anything truly traumatic. She'd blacked out as much from the fall itself as the impact, but that was short-lived. She had sustained worse injuries over the years, and she judged this was nothing a few more minutes of cold compression and a couple of over-the-counter pills couldn't fix.

"Do you have any ibuprofen?"

"We're not supposed to give oral medicine to patients." Iris spoke as if she were reading from a safety manual. "It's against regulation."

"But dispensing yogurt is fine?" Danica couldn't help prodding with her words, though Iris seemed to ignore them.

"Iris," Dr. Urban addressed his technician, "could you bring Miss Lara a bottle of water? There are some cold ones in the back of the fridge."

"Yes, Dr. Urban." Iris spun on her heel and exited the examination room, leaving Danica alone with Dr. Urban.

He immediately lowered his voice. "You can rip open that yogurt if you like. No harm, no foul."

Danica looked at him, seeing him for the first time. A light expression lit his alabaster face, bright eyes of blue staring back at her. His short, blond hair was in stark contrast to his black rimmed hipster glasses. He looked something like a reset version of a superhero alter-ego, half comic book hero and half Norseman. His unique features made him stand out in a bold way. "I do like yogurt. And I didn't expect a snack from my first visit to the optometrist."

"About that," Dr. Urban's tone segued into what Danica imagined was his exam mode. "So you've never had a visual exam?"

"Not really. I had something in grade school."

"And then?"

"That was it. I read a chart, got an all-clear diagnosis from the school nurse, and went back to class."

Dr. Urban cocked his head, a sinewy muscle tightening on his neck that Danica followed until the length of it disappeared somewhere beneath the collar of his white medical jacket. Perhaps other muscles as taut were hidden beneath that same fabric—but Danica snapped her focus back to his questions.

"So what brings you in today?"

"Trouble seeing things up close." She paused,

realizing the irony. "I guess you could say like a big brick wall."

"Absolutely not. You weren't expecting that column to be where it was. I told the architect that leaving it in place was a bad decision, but he insisted."

"Was your architect Roland Reinhardt?"

Dr. Urban blinked his surprise. "How did you know?"

"I work at the appraisal district office. I know all the area architects and builders. And a fair share of the framers, stone masons, and electricians too. I know who just bought property, who is getting ready to sell property, and the list of businesses who are always late paying their taxes."

"Duly noted. I'll make sure I never make that list."

"Haven't seen you on it yet. But you've only had this place on the appraisal rolls for a little over a year." Danica knew of the location long before the sign was hung outside announcing the new business to passersby. "And you got some good tax breaks, too, from the Economic Development Corporation."

"That's right." He leaned back as if meeting his match. "You seem to know a lot about me."

"I know absolutely nothing about you," Danica corrected. "Other than you are Dr. Grady Urban doing business as Spectacle Optique."

Grady extended his hand. "Then allow me to introduce myself. Grady Urban, DBA Spectacle Optique. You can call me Grady. And I'm a big fan of small towns, one-on-one conversations, and frozen yogurt pops."

Danica raised her hand to meet his "Danica Lara. I like long walks on the beach, warm sunsets, and walking into brick walls." After such a hard fall, this conversation felt like a soft landing.

As they finished a handshake, she lifted her hand to massage her temple.

"Still bothering you?" Grady's gentle tone held concern that Danica could sense even without looking directly at him.

Considering she'd been nervous before this appointment and had made a fool of herself by landing on her back before the actual examination even got off the ground, she would say that, yes, she was still bothered. But she was sure that wasn't exactly what Dr. Urban was asking.

Danica was spared the spotlight of an answer as Iris reentered the room, pert and springy with an outstretched bottle of water. "Found one. Nice and cool."

"Thank you." Danica accepted the water and now juggled the bottle, her purse, and the yogurt pop. "I didn't expect food and drink at the optometrist."

"And to think I only registered this as a medical business." Dr. Urban snapped his fingers in a dramatic aw-shucks move. "Should have also made it clear this was an afternoon improv club with snack bar."

"So what's your next act?" Danica prompted.

Dr. Urban lifted the sleeve of his medical coat to check the time, his finger striking his smart watch awake. "Considering I had thirty minutes blocked for you but we've already used up almost half of that, I could have you speed read some eye charts and make a too-quick assessment of your vision." He didn't sound the least bit convincing. "Or I can grab another yogurt pop, and we can share an afternoon snack while you tell me more about Seguin."

That wasn't what she expected from a doctor. Was he wanting to see possible side effects from her blackout, or was he wanting to use the time to get to know her for a more personal reason? Danica's thoughts were as rusty as her experience in romantic relationships. "What about my actual appointment?"

"Let's let your head clear, and we'll reschedule that." He turned to glance over his shoulder. "Iris, can you tell Samantha to work with Miss Lara for any time she is available later in the week?" Grady turned his attention again to Danica. Pushing his glasses back onto the bridge of his nose, he addressed her as if they were the only two in the room. "I needed an afternoon break anyway."

~*~

Danica hadn't expected to spend a portion of her afternoon in a dim examination room chatting in private with Dr. Grady Urban. She was left with a small bump on her forehead, a reminder card for her new appointment at end-of-day Friday, and a cagey feeling in the pit of her stomach, which she couldn't shake.

Back at the appraisal district office, she stationed herself at her cubicle for the rest of the afternoon. She reset her digital phone message, opened her e-mail, and made herself available to whatever crisis would arise next. There was always a fire of one kind or another to put out in the office.

Her language skills were also prized because she was bilingual in English and Spanish, having grown up in a household with a Mexican father. So she was often called for translation services, and she knew of one such case that she needed to organize for the following morning.

Since there was a full slate of Appraisal Review Board hearings she would have to attend the next day, she decided to use what was left of her afternoon to return messages and make preparations. She latched her fingers beneath the edge of her desk to pull her roller chair closer. The pesky computer screen's lettering appeared to shrink daily. She checked the computer's resolution.

"Nope," Danica muttered. "It's not you. It's me." She heaved a sigh, unable to blame technology for the fuzziness she saw. That was a result of her own vision, and now she'd have to wait two more days to get a proper answer from Dr. Grady Urban. Why were the simplest of tasks complicated as of late?

She had no choice but to bite back her pride, keep her head close to the screen, and do her work as best she could.

Deep in thought and distracted by digital waves that Danica generally didn't see on spreadsheets, her concentration was broken by a co-worker. "How'd the appointment go?" She looked up to see Trish leaning over the top of her cubicle.

Danica kept her head low and finger-combed her bangs to the side to camouflage the bump. Then, like the speed of a key-strike, her mouth fired an automatic response of "Fine."

"Do you need glasses?"

"Probably." Danica couldn't imagine she'd get a clean bill of eye health, especially since she could measure the distance between her and her computer screen in inches, not feet. "I don't know yet."

"You didn't get screened?" Trish's eyes held perfect vision. She had never so much as used eyedrops, as far as Danica knew.

"I have to go back Friday."

"Sounds good." But it's not like Trish had any basis for understanding that. "By the way, while you were out, Barry came by."

"Barry Van Soyt?"

Trish rolled her eyes. "Who else?"

"Did he leave a note?"

Trish shook her head. "He said he would text you."

Danica needed to remind Barry to stop coming by without professional cause. True, they were partnering together on a business venture to develop a plot of land near the edge of town as Cinnamon Ridge Estates, but Danica needed to deepen the divide between office time and her personal time. "Thanks, Trish."

Trish lingered. She pulled at a strand of her hair and twirled it around her finger. "He's lost some weight you know. In the stomach."

"I hadn't noticed."

"He looks good. Better, you know?"

Danica didn't. She wasn't interested in the changing physique of her best friend's ex-husband. After Barry's divorce from Paige, Danica had entered into an acreage development agreement with him, and in hindsight, even though she was only doing it because it was a smart land opportunity, it did temporarily muddy the waters of their friendship. But Danica had addressed that with Paige, and now she just wanted to finish subdividing the property, develop basic subdivision infrastructure, and get the lots on the market. Once the project saw fruition, she hoped to walk away with a profit.

"How old is he?" Trish mused as her eyes turned to glass.

"Look," Danica removed her hands from the keyboard, turning squarely to Trish. "I know you think it might be fun to start a relationship with Barry—"

"Danica!" Trish leveled a cool scold that Danica knew was for show. Trish was desperate for any man who had boyfriend potential, even if he wasn't exactly the hottest commodity on the market.

"But, trust me, Barry Van Soyt has his head in business. That's it."

"Maybe a man that level-headed is exactly what I need." She lifted her chin.

"That's not Barry. Besides, what you need is not a middle-aged, recently divorced man who's consumed by projects. That's not exactly the picture of relationship bliss."

"I don't need relationship bliss. I just need...a relationship."

Way to aim high. "I wouldn't say he's a good candidate for a romantic relationship. I'm not going to set you up with him."

"I didn't ask you to."

She didn't have to. Trish may have thought she was being subtle, however, she was anything but.

"What's it to you anyway?" Trish twirled away at her hair. "You involved with him?"

Danica sighed with the weight of misunderstanding. And that was exactly why her partnership with Barry needed to come to an end. "We have one project going. That's it." Hardly an involvement, in the general sense of the word. "No dinners, no rendezvous. Absolutely no romance."

Trish separated her finger from her twirl of hair, the strand springing back into place with enviable tensile strength that Danica typically only saw on shampoo commercials. "Well, he knows where to find me."

"Yes. He does." This was Seguin, after all, a small enough town where there wasn't much place to hide.

Not from professional projects, like her one with Barry.

And not even from botched appointments, like her one with Dr. Urban.

As Trish left, Danica brought her hand to her head again, massaging the spot of impact and wondering if the pain building beneath her temple was from her fall or from stressors in her life in general.

Danica resumed her computer work, hoping to minimize the distraction by being productive. That usually worked.

One hour, two cups of water, and three spreadsheets later, Danica was finding her groove again, sailing through the afternoon and getting everything organized for the following day. A cell phone ping from her purse caught her attention just as she was about to leave her desk for the copy machine.

She slid open the bottom drawer of her desk where she stashed her red leather purse. Holding the phone in one hand, she thumbed the screen and read a text from Barry that indicated a problem with the water line placement in Cinnamon Ridge. The text ended with CALL ME.

NOT NOW, she responded back. Then, in a follow-up, just to make it clear to him that she wasn't interested in getting involved during her work hours, she added, HANDLE IT.

Danica was ready to stash her phone back into her purse when it pinged again. THEN WILL YOU BE THE ONE TO TELL POTENTIAL HOMEBUYERS THEY DON'T HAVE OUTDOOR FAUCETS?

"What in the world?" Danica muttered. She set the phone on her desk to prevent her from throwing it across the room. This was exactly the type of involvement in the project she could no longer stand. She never anticipated this level of weekly—sometimes daily—involvement with infrastructure setup. And two people were supposed to make this easier, not harder.

While Danica thought of what to say next, Barry filled the phone screen. ATTRACTIVE LOTS = BIG PROFITS followed by NO WATER = NOT ATTRACTIVE.

AS IF I NEEDED YOU TO POINT THAT OUT. Surely, whatever engineering puzzle he was referring to could be fixed. When it came to land development, there was always a way. Barry just needed to buck-up and take charge because Danica didn't have time for this. She tapped her fingers on the edge of her desk, thinking of the best way to persuade him of that. And then it came to her.

WANT ME TO CALL EVERETT?

Nothing was as emasculating to Barry Van Soyt as a reference to his ex-wife's new husband. Everett Mullins had brought his high skill as a water well driller and water consultant back to the Seguin area after his marriage to Danica's best friend, Paige. The triangle of friend, ex, and new husband was a thorny one, but Danica knew the offer would work to silence Barry tight as a clam shell.

And it did, with the exception of a simple I'LL MAKE IT WORK, which is exactly what Danica wanted in the first place. When trouble arose, people just needed to find a way to rise, too.

She stashed her phone back in her purse, slid the drawer shut, and grabbed a slim stack of papers to head to the copy machine. She tallied the number of sets she needed as she walked, placed the papers in the tray, and punched in her code.

"Danica!" Trish called over the noise of the machine. "Call the city manager."

She turned to meet her coworker. "What now?"

Trish's face soured as she explained a toilet backup in the women's bathroom. "We need a plumber. Bad."

It was one surprise after another. The pain in her temple built again.

The office needed a plumber. Cinnamon Ridge needed an engineer. Her eyes needed an exam...and her body really needed a masseuse.

THREE

Late Friday afternoon, Danica sat in Spectacle Optique.

"That's the only kind I'll wear," a teenager argued with her mother about wanting cat eye contacts.

"Over my dead body." The mother didn't even look up from her cell phone when she answered.

"That's not fair," the teen pouted.

The mother mumbled something about life that Danica couldn't hear, probably some adage. The woman continued to bury her head in her screen, an odd generational reversal that Danica considered from her position across the waiting room. Like the rows of eyeglasses, she couldn't help but continue to watch.

"I don't know anyone in my grade who has them." The teenager's appeal to popularity was laced with longing.

Tap, tap, tap. "Maybe there's a reason."

"Mom," she whined, a low-bellowed vocal tug that made Danica herself want to give in to her importunities. "You told me that when I was old enough—"

"You're not old enough." The mother finally tore her eyes from her screen long enough to shut her daughter down with, "end of story."

The daughter crossed her arms, huffed, and leaned back into her chair, setting her shoulder at an angle to her mother.

Danica wanted to tell the girl there were probably some cat eye frames she could choose instead. But she kept her mouth shut. She had done enough talking today, and her lips were as tired as her eyes.

Iris entered the room a few minutes later and called the girl back. "I'll wait here," her mom said before resuming her digital tap, tap, tap.

Danica closed her eyes, the cell phone tapping like a metronome in the otherwise quiet space. She thought about her own vision. If it was needed, would she opt for glasses or contacts? Hearing the daughter mention cat eyes prompted Danica to daydream about changing her own brown eyes into something with a splash more color. Like trying a new hairstyle, a change could be a lot of fun.

Her mind ruminated on options she could only imagine since she didn't even know the state of her vision.

But she soon would. After ten minutes passed, Iris appeared with a clipboard and called Danica from the doorway, déjà vu of two days earlier. "Let's get you started back here."

Danica grabbed her purse and stepped across the waiting room to the beat of the digital tap, tap, tap. "Hi again," she greeted Iris. "I'm going to take the hallway turn very carefully this time." She paced as if in momentary slow motion.

Iris ushered her inside with an outstretched hand.

"Sounds like you remember the column around the corner."

"How could I forget?"

"It looks good to me." Iris touched her fingers to her forehead in gesture to Danica's sore spot. "No bump?"

The memory of that was still green. "It's gone down." But beneath Danica's bangs, there was a light yellow-brown bruise that was still a bit sensitive to the touch.

"Dr. Urban will be glad to hear that." Iris walked around Danica to lead the way into the examination room.

"Oh?"

"Yes." She pushed the door forward and held it open for them both. "He was really worried."

"That was kind of him." Danica pulled her purse to the front of her.

"That's how he is." Iris had a dreamy look in her eyes. "Always thoughtful."

Danica bit her lip, unsure how to respond to what felt like a private daydream a little too close for shared comfort. Maybe the young blonde had a thing for her boss.

"Well," Iris cleared her throat. "Let's talk about your eyes instead. How can the doctor help you today?" And with that, Iris reset into appointment mode with Danica as her focus.

~*~

Grady found himself again debating the merits of function over form. "Skylar," he told the teen who sat pout-lipped in his exam chair. "I can't make your mother buy you cat eye contacts."

"But you could suggest it." She kept her arms crossed over her chest, a look of misplaced autonomy across her countenance that only years of teenage practice could perfect.

"I write prescriptions." Grady kept his voice level and dictatorial. "I don't make fashion suggestions."

"But," she insisted, drawing out the syllable, "you can tell my mom that you sell those kind of contacts."

"They can be special ordered," he conceded. "Cat eyes, spiraling pupils, zombie whiteouts—"

"Did you say zombie?" Her interest piqued with more pep than a high school cheerleader.

"Optometry possibilities are vast." That's one reason he loved the field. "I can special order pretty much anything you want." He corrected himself before Skylar could run with his words. "I mean, anything your mother wants you to have."

"She won't let me have anything." The pouty lower lip made its appearance again.

Grady still needed practice with teenagers. Iris and Samantha were both closer in age to them. Maybe he would ask them for tips to ease communication with this generation he felt a world away from now that he was in his thirties.

He scribbled a note on Skylar's chart. "How about I have Samantha make you a copy of your prescription? You can take it home, talk to your mom, and come back here to order contacts, glasses, or both when you're ready."

"She doesn't change her mind too often," she mumbled.

To Grady, that didn't sound like a bad parenting trait. "Anything else you want to ask me?"

Skylar slid a sly gaze to Grady. "I do want to ask if you have a thing for your assistant."

Grady stilled his hand and lowered his head. He looked at Skylar over the top rim of his glasses. "Excuse me?"

"Because she has a thing for you." Skylar uncrossed her arms and leaned forward slightly in the examination chair as she nosed her way into his private life.

"We're not going to discuss this." Employee impropriety was not a rumor he wanted to start. Nor did he want to give any reason to fan the flames of local gossip, especially as they related to some teenager's misplaced fantasy. "We work together. And we work for our patients."

Skylar snorted. "She's working on something else as far as I can see..."

Grady kept a straight face. He had nothing to hide. "Any other questions? About your eyes?"

With Grady's refusal to crack his veneer of professionalism, Skylar's dilated pupils became voids of disinterest. "No, I guess not."

He grabbed a set of rolled-up post-appointment eye shields. "Since your eyes were dilated, light is going to seem intense when you step out of this room and especially when you go outside. Wear these for the next hour or so."

Skylar unrolled the wrap-around shields and fitted them as she would a pair of sunglasses. "Fashionable," she quipped.

"You'll be the talk of SHS if you wear those past today." Grady volleyed back his own version of light humor. He rose from his seat to switch on the light overhead which had been dimmed during her exam.

"I'm already the talk of my high school." Skylar spoke softly from behind him, a sadness in her words that Grady felt even without looking at her.

Grady was no therapist, but even he sensed the sorrow of those words. Teen reality was a crowded cafeteria of emotions. He didn't always know what to say with some of his patients, especially those who were underage. But he was too caring to say nothing. "It gets better," he offered.

"Maybe." Skylar's exam was over, and so was this conversation. She didn't thank him on the way out, but Grady wasn't a doctor who needed special gestures of gratitude.

But he did need to find a way to connect with patients who needed extra hand holding, if only for the short time they were in his office. That bit of business operation was something he'd have to continue to exercise if he wanted to keep and attract clientele of all ages, especially in this area where word of mouth could damage a new business's reputation.

Happy clients meant happy appointments. Happy appointments meant a healthy bottom line to Spectacle

Optique's balance sheet. And at such an early stage in his new business, he needed to keep his eye on that.

Danica Lara was his last appointment for the day, and with profit and loss on his mind, he gently wanted to find out about her forehead bump from Wednesday. The possibility of a lawsuit, even if remote, was one he wanted to keep at bay. Nothing would sink his finances faster than unnecessary legal expenses.

He passed the second exam room where Danica was inside just as Iris was coming out.

"Hi," she breathed low as she tugged the door closed behind her. "Just finishing up." She extended the clipboard to Grady before returning both hands behind her back. Her chest popped more than was normal for a standing position.

Intentional? Skylar's words regarding Iris's flirty intentions echoed in Grady's ears. He looked down at the chart, diverting his gaze to read the patient notes. Out of the corner of his eye, he saw Iris lengthen her torso in a cool display of seduction.

"Any questions for me?" She leaned in close to Grady, the curves of her body within range to touch. If he dared.

He didn't.

"No."

Iris twisted at the waist, a sway of concentrated interest lingering. "I'll see you after the appointment then."

Iris was a gorgeous girl, and she was a solid employee. His tight group of employees—including Heath who ran the retail optical side—all worked well together. And he didn't want to rock that boat. Not by responding to any flirty lines cast by Iris or by sending the wrong message with any responsive behavior.

Not that a single doctor in a new town didn't have hopes.

He was a full-bodied male with interest in the opposite sex. His single status made him a target for women looking for a prospective boyfriend. But he had no intention of mixing business with pleasure or jeopardizing all that he worked hard to build.

Summoning the same firm voice he used with Skylar, he thanked Iris for her work and made no eye contact with her as he led with the clipboard, sidestepped her body, and walked into his final appointment for the week.

Whereas Iris held herself with pride and stood in close proximity to Grady, Danica seemed to retreat within herself the moment Grady pulled his stool nearer to the exam chair.

"I'm not used to having someone so close," she explained when he instructed her to settle her chin into place so he could use the equipment for examining her eyes.

Now Grady felt as if he were having a complete role reversal from the hallway. But unlike Iris, there was a necessity to his proximity. He used words to lighten the mood. "I just want to have a good look at those sparklers."

"I don't know how sparkly they are." Danica repositioned her chin and rested her forehead against the arched piece of metal to which Grady pointed for stability. "But you can have a look."

Grady pushed back his glasses, letting the magnification inside of the lens do the work for him. Seeing a patient's eyes up close was one of his preferred parts of the job. "Brown eyes are my favorite."

"Oh, I bet you say that to all the girls."

Danica blinked through Grady's stare, which he knew she couldn't see through the slit lamp between them.

"You caught me," he admitted in jest. "But if you can stay still a bit longer, I can have a proper look."

Danica obliged, staying silent as her eyes did the talking for her.

And, oh, the story they told.

Grady always took longer than most optometrists during this part of an exam. "I'm checking these from top to bottom." Grady kept his own head and gaze steady. "I want to make sure I give enough attention to all parts of these hard-working eyes."

His care in examining allowed him to adjust to nuances he saw that a cursory overview didn't catch. For most people, looking into eyes returned the look of a single hue, like brown or blue or green. But when he looked at eyes, he saw something more complex. Each part of the eye glistened in nuanced shades that may be sensory overload to anyone else. However, Grady loved this line of work and embraced what he could uncover by looking into these parts of another person that were so private.

In Danica, he saw brown streaked with gold and

amber rays, flecks of honey-hued lines accented by shadows more colorful than an artist's palette. Like a microbrewer might be skilled at recognizing different grades of alcohol by the color of the liquid, Grady's eyes were hypersensitive to the point of seeing what others missed.

But as he looked deep into Danica's eyes, he got lost in their beauty. Looking at her was a glorious detour into enjoying the pleasures of his career field.

He stared.

She stared.

And he nearly forgot the reason why he was looking at her in the first place.

FOUR

Danica was fully clothed, so why did she suddenly feel completely exposed?

She tugged at the edge of her blouse, rubbing her fingers against the hem of the fabric as an outlet for nerves that came out of nowhere. True, she had been nervous the first time she stepped into Spectacle Optique.

But not like this.

This level of tension was tinged with something more primal and personal than white glove fear of a doctor. Even without words, she revealed more than if she had completed a multi-page medical questionnaire or full-body examination.

Dr. Urban was looking at a part of her that no one had ever looked at before.

At least not like this.

Being on the receiving end of his magnified attention, she did as she was told. She kept her head steady, her eyelids opened, and her focus tight. His eyes were looking directly into hers, but she couldn't see through the machinery that separated them.

Instead, her other senses kicked into high gear.

Dr. Urban had a sharp, clean scent, like a new bar of soap. If it were cologne or antiseptic hand cleaner responsible for the aroma, Danica wasn't sure. Its effect was immediate, almost like awakening to smelling salts. She didn't know she could be invigorated by an office visit to an optometrist.

Or that her heart could somersault from a feeling that had lain dormant so long. The flip-flop of her insides was a giddy reminder that she was a woman with physical sensations that may have just needed a little jolt. Like a reminder of what was dominant in her twenties, Danica's body was telling her not to forget what it could do. She was a woman in her thirties who could attract the attention of a man.

If she was interested.

Was she? Danica privately considered the idea. She hadn't recently entertained male attention in her life, not with her responsibilities at work and since the development project with Barry demanded nearly all her energy. Barry had—in a completely misplaced way—tried to dangle a thread of flirtation in front of her just for kicks, and that had soured her on trying anything with a man, at least for the short term. She chalked up his actions to post-divorce desperation, and all their encounters since had been project-centered.

Still, she knew this feeling.

Or she thought she did.

She continued rubbing the hem of her blouse as she stayed on display, if only through her eyes. She dared not ask him what he saw.

Danica tried untangling her frenzy of thoughts from the quiet reality in which she sat. She was in a dark room, within inches of a gorgeous man. Alone.

Of course, she felt giddy. If Danica were used to such encounters, she'd have no reason to feel the sensuous tingles that crept over her. Maybe it was anxiety again. She flashed back to her heightened nerves on Wednesday, a flashback of her fainting spell that reminded her of her weakness. She didn't do well with doctors who might deliver a diagnosis that would change something about her status quo. Even if it were just a prescription for corrective lenses, Danica was typically in charge when it came to her well-being. This part of her health wasn't something she could control, and that made her uncertain.

Anxious.

Lightheaded.

The sensation from Wednesday hit again.

"Miss Lara?" Dr. Urban pulled back from the machine. He brought his glasses back into place and pushed his heels against the floor as the stool swung to place him within view of Danica. "Are you feeling all right?"

Vertiginous as a bad tightrope walk roper, Danica replied, "Fine."

Dr. Urban extended his hand atop her free one to quell her nervousness. The fingers of her other hand were rubbing so hard against her shirt fabric that she was on-track to tear a hole through it.

"Let's get that breathing back in check," he coached. "Follow my lead." He inhaled and exhaled with a measured rhythm that Danica tried to match. She needed oxygen to reach her brain for sure.

"In..." Dr. Urban's chest broadened beneath his

white coat as he filled his lungs. "And out." He dropped his shoulders and expended what he held. "And again."

Danica followed his lead, but her cadence was not as controlled as his. Still, she tried to brush away the severity with another "I'm fine" that sounded as hallow as it really was.

"Humor me." He smiled. "In," he breathed again, "and out."

She did as she was told, although her head still felt like it was five stories above the seat where she sat.

Dr. Urban leaned in, coaching more explicitly with a quiet demand. "Look at me."

She locked eyes with this man whose skin in contact with hers sent a warm shock through her. Now his raw gaze met her in a transcendent space that made her heart pump in strong bursts that she controlled— by deep breaths.

In.

And out.

Dr. Urban had met Danica where she was and brought her to where she needed to be. Within moments, she was back in control.

And back to absolute vulnerability in front of the gaze of a man whom she wanted to look at longer than her appointment would allow.

"Is that better?" His eyes shone with the sincerity of his words.

"Much." Danica nodded.

Oh, Dr. Urban was good. If all doctors were like him, Danica might seek medical care more often.

~*~

"Do you want the good news first or the bad news?" Grady Urban grabbed his clipboard as Danica settled back into the exam chair. Delivering results was something he did differently with different patients. With Danica, he opted to give her a choice in how to hear what he needed to say.

"The good." Danica was still adjusting to the sensation of her eye examination: the series of lenses, the bright blue light up close, the eye drops that made a strange yellow discharge against a tissue with which she had to dab, and then the questions. Her eyes were as fatigued as the rest of her forty-hour-work-week body. "Hit me with it."

"You came in complaining of fuzziness in your vision. And it's treatable. No major problems at all. You just need corrective lenses."

"Glasses?"

"Or contacts," Grady clarified. "Entirely your call."

Danica nodded her understanding. "Now the bad news?"

Grady's jaw tightened. "I'm sorry to say I have no cat eye contacts in stock if that's what you were wanting."

Danica cracked a smile. "I suspect another patient of yours did."

Grady brought his hand to his chin, rubbing it with the memory of Skylar. "I guess you heard her in the waiting room?"

"I practically heard her through the walls."

That was an aspect of the remodel for which he hadn't splurged. Perhaps a little more insulation inside the drywall would have helped. Small regrets such as this crept in week after week since the shop opened. He was concerned with patient privacy, but he miscalculated how loud people in the area talked. Was that a dialect difference or a socialized difference? No use worrying about it now. What was spent, was spent. "Sorry about that."

"Don't apologize." Danica flipped her hair over her shoulder, tucking it between her body and the back of the chair. "You should hear my office."

"Loud?"

"More than you would think."

Maybe people in this town were just loud talkers.

Grady lay his clipboard atop his lap. "So, back to your eyewear choices."

"Yes. Eyewear." Danica heaved a sigh. "I'm in my thirties, and I'm getting my first pair of glasses."

Grady helped customers of all ages, but he understood that any patient's first set of eyewear was a significant event. "So, no contacts then?"

"No." Danica shrugged, drawing her gaze to the dead center between his eyes where his glasses stretched across the bridge of his nose. "You don't wear contacts."

"True." Grady pushed back his glasses so that they sat a touch higher. "But don't let that influence you."

Danica tucked back the other side of her hair, this time shaking her head ever so slightly to keep the hair long and loose behind her. Her countenance was pretty in one of those ways that only a woman who knew herself could carry. Someone who was comfortable in her skin and had a way about her that he admired. It was different than someone like Iris, who was perky and persistent in ways that weren't always welcomed. Danica held a coolness, a maturity that matched his own age. "When do I have to pick out glasses?"

"That's entirely up to you. And you can get them here, but I'm obliged to tell you that you can take this prescription to any optical shop." He handed her a single sheet of paper with his signature on the bottom.

"But you'd like me to shop here?"

"As a new business, yes." Grady swallowed his pride, knowing he needed the patronage however he could get it. "I would like you to consider getting glasses from here."

Danica folded the sheet of paper in a neat line across its middle. "Done deal. I'll look on the way out."

"You may want to wait on that." He handed Danica a set of rolled-up post-appointment eye shields. "Keep these on for the next hour or so until your eyes adjust to the light. It's going to seem a little disorienting to look up close, so it's best you shop for frames when those sparklers are a bit more ready for it. That'll take about an hour, and it's late. Why don't you plan on coming in Monday?"

Danica unrolled the shields and stretched them wide as she lifted them to her face, settling them into place... upside down.

"Um," Grady lifted a finger into the air. "May I

suggest—"

"A more attractive choice of sunglasses?" Danica jostled him in a playful way. "Yes, absolutely you can."

"How about we try this?" Grady inched his stool nearer to Danica, lifted his hands to each side of her face, and cupped the edge of the eye shields. He righted them before gingerly replacing them so they sat as they should.

Danica's cheeks flushed. Whether the hue was from embarrassment or from the brush of Grady's touch, he wasn't certain.

What he was certain about was that the close contact—even though it was something he did every day with patients—was different with Danica. And though the room was still slightly dark, he was sure his cheeks were flushing too.

What an odd sensation to have such a ripple move through him. Grady was squarely focused on making his business a success. That was his main goal in Seguin, not chasing a courtship. Personal desires were on the back burner.

~*~

Danica's second trip to the optometrist now netted a third trip.

Bump on the head, examination of the eyes, and frame selection for her face. Who knew pursuit of medical attention for one body part could result in such a flurry of appointments?

So Danica took her prescription, thanked Dr.

Urban, and walked out of Spectacle Optique. With dilated eyes, she stepped off the curb and into a blaze of late afternoon light more vibrant than a solar eclipse.

"Intense," she whistled through her teeth, a bit shaky on her feet. She walked along the side of her car and was glad for the bit of reprieve as she settled herself behind the driver's seat. She started the ignition, and her car roared to life as her eyes squinted behind the dark shields that she was thankful now covered her eyes. Altered sight was a dizzying state.

At home, she managed to park and navigate her way inside, not wanting to remove the eye shields even when she entered. She kept every light off. A quiet and dim Friday night wasn't originally on her agenda, but that was her reality.

Danica dropped her purse at the edge of her couch. She kicked off her shoes, swung her legs horizontally, and perched lazily with her feet hanging just over the edge of the couch's arm. She draped a hand over the side, letting her fingers muscle-memory their way across the subtle leather sides of her purse and into the cloth recesses to where her phone lay stashed inside.

She brought the phone before her face, punching the contrast down the moment it came on. Everything was still so bright. She scrolled to Paige's name and pushed the call through so that she could commiserate with her best friend.

"I need glasses."

"Well, hello to you, too."

"I mean it. I'm actually a woman who has lived

three decades on the earth, and my body is starting to turn on me."

"Don't you think that's a little dramatic?" Paige's motherly tone was one she usually reserved for her son, Nathan, but every once in a while, she managed to direct it toward Danica.

"I am a single woman alone on a Friday night. On my sofa. And I'm like some kind of vampire who can't stand the light."

"Eyes dilated?"

"How did you know?" Danica reached her hand to the corner of the eye shields, adjusting them once more against her face.

"That's what happens at the eye doctor."

Danica was like a teenager oblivious to the cool kids' table in the cafeteria. "Does everyone know this but me?"

"Part of my knowledge base," Paige responded.

"Even though you don't wear glasses?"

"I've still been to the eye doctor."

"You have?" How did Danica not know this about her friend?

"A couple of years ago. And one time in college."

"And?" Danica prompted for more information.

"Nothing to say. Examination and a 20/20 vision diagnosis. End of story."

"Show off," Danica rebuked. "I know you have good vision, but I didn't know you've had eye exams." She thought she knew everything about Paige.

"No big deal."

Danica envisioned her friend sloughing off the

comment with a flip of her hair over her shoulder.

"But it's something I didn't know about you."

"Well, now you know." Paige's experience as a mother continued to shine through her nonchalant tone. "Besides, you're older than me—"

"Only by two months!" If Paige were in the same room with her, she would have shouldered her in a physical jab to match the verbal one. "Don't make me sound older than I am."

"You are not old. Neither of us is."

Danica certainly didn't feel that way. "I have a bump on my head. I fell at the doctor's office the first time I went."

"Danica!" Now Paige's voice rose with concern that wasn't a joke. "You didn't tell me that!"

"It's my age. Maybe I forgot."

"Be serious." Paige's sincerity shift was immediate. "You fell? Do you mean tripped? Fell down to the ground? Or what?"

There was no fanfare for what happened. "Bumped my head. Landed flat on my back. Had to be helped up."

"Did you get doctored by the doctor?"

"If only he was more than an eye specialist. He gave me yogurt."

Silence.

More silence.

"Paige?" Danica made sure her friend was still there.

"Why did he do that?"

Danica reviled, her face souring in response. "To

ice my head."

"OK." Paige clipped their conversation. "I've got Nathan in the background here. I'm about to get dinner ready. Are you going to be OK tonight?"

"Yes, I'll be fine." Danica pushed her melodrama aside.

"Even knowing you will always age before me?"

"Two. Months."

"Still..."

"Fine, fine, fine." This was usually how their conversations went. Seriousness juxtaposed with banter that only women who were friends for years and years could navigate.

"Call me tomorrow? Or later if that bump on your head gets any worse?"

"I'm past that." Danica reached above her temple, feeling the slight rise of her skin. "Just nursing the swelling."

"Ouch. That must have been some fall."

Danica rubbed the spot with a light touch. "Too bad I didn't quite land in the arms of the doctor."

"Oooh!" Paige dished. "You didn't tell me about Dr. McHottie. Is he as hot-hot as everyone says?"

"You're a married woman," Danica reminded her friend.

"You haven't answered my question."

"Do you use language like that around your husband?"

"Dr. McHottie?" Paige dismissed any concern with the reality that Danica knew to be true of her forever friend. "I love my husband. Everett knows he has my heart. And my wanton attention." Paige added, "Now you, on the other hand..."

"Don't you start." Paige had tried to set up Danica in the past. But having a happily-married friend play matchmaker was a lot quainter in theory than practice.

"He's single, right?" Paige asked of Seguin's latest addition to the medical field.

"As far as I know." Danica hadn't heard anything to the contrary. "No ring."

Paige squealed. "So you looked!"

Danica was caught in her gotcha moment. "I may have been guilty of taking a peek."

Paige cooed a happy valuation. "He's available!"

She certainly meant well—she always did—but Paige, who was settled in what Danica saw to be perfect marital and family bliss, was a bit too eager to edge her friend into that direction. "I'll think about it."

"I bet you will." Paige's words were as sly as a sideways wink.

But as Danica ended the call with her friend, she was hit with the reality of being alone on a Friday night. Not a man in sight, and a rather slim prospect of one when it came to actually making a move toward interest in Dr. Urban, a man in front of whom she had already embarrassed herself and with whom she had little reason to interact, beyond seeking his optometry care. He cared for patients' eyes, but Danica couldn't see someone so focused in his field falling for any emotion of the heart.

FIVE

Being single had advantages and disadvantages.

Danica was definitely enjoying some of the advantages this weekend. First, there was zero melodrama. She enjoyed time to herself—which is what she always had, thanks to her single status—but on weekends like this one, she reveled in doing activities only as she wanted.

Sure, Paige had Everett and Nathan. But a husband and son also meant responsibilities. And fulfilling certain expectations. Quite simply, there were roles that Paige had to play that Danica didn't in the least.

So when Danica decided that she wanted a midmorning nap, she took one.

And when she decided to eat ice cream for lunch on Saturday, she did.

Then when she tidied up her house and sorted laundry in the afternoon, she decided to do so in a sports bra and pajama bottoms.

There was no one to stop her.

But a few disadvantages reared their ugly head, too.

For instance, when she curled on the couch to watch a Saturday night movie marathon of her favorite trilogy, she had to do so alone. And watching a romance develop between the hero and heroine made her a bit lonely.

Being accountable to no one had its perks, but being alone had its downsides too.

Debating the merits of which one of the three films was the best or most romantic also had to take place alone. And there was little fun in having an internal argument with herself. Danica halted her thoughts, determined not to reduce her singledom into a pathetic one-sided conversation that had no merits other than passing the time. And if she really wanted a reason to do that, she should save such thoughts for work when the hours lazed on and she needed a mental distraction.

Danica's only distraction now needed to be something a tad more productive. The weekends were the only time she was completely free to focus on her own responsibilities outside of the appraisal district. After the movie, she padded to her corner desk, pulled out the chair, and sat as she flipped open the pages of her personal calendar.

Danica scanned the squares that comprised the month's page. Taking inventory of the days ahead, she made a quick list of things she needed to do during the week, including time to shop for glasses back at Spectacle Optique. Maybe over Tuesday's lunch hour? Or Wednesday? Those were possibilities. Danica perused the rest of the days of the week, seeing a scratch of pencil script on Friday with the letters "SES" followed by "8:15 a.m."

She tugged at the memory of what she was reading, trying to recall the reason for those letters and numbers. Usually, she was keen when it came to recollection. That was, after all, her reason for keeping a paper calendar. While many people relied on a digital one, Danica's habit of writing could not be broken. In the simple act of writing, she found that she had greater memory, retention, and commitment to projects than when she absently typed them into a digital screen that she could minimize from physical view.

Except for this moment.

"SES?" She said the letters aloud, hoping their taste on her tongue would spark a memory.

Nothing.

Maybe that bump on her head was affecting her far more than she thought.

~*~

Grady's weekend was glitz and glamour.

For a good cause.

Twinkling lights adorned the ceiling in billowy rows interspersed with tulle, creating a cozy white canopy above the space of the community hall for the Guadalupe County Medical Center's annual benefit gala. Wrought iron accent pieces staged between lush tropical plants and colorful streamers broke the otherwise monochromatic vast interior. Candlelight danced in controlled bursts while people ebbed among one another, the pale light casting shadows.

The contrasts toyed with Grady. He squinted then briefly shut his eyes when he needed momentary rest from the bustle of the scenes and colors. To anyone else, he probably just looked like he was fighting allergies.

But even the eyes of an optometrist needed a break.

Aside from visual adjustment, he was also more of an introvert by nature and only an extrovert by virtue of his career choice. But there were people with whom he should mingle at this event, so he couldn't stay closed off from them.

As if on cue, an open palm landed on Grady's shoulder, the bearer giving it a squeeze of welcome. "Good to see you, Dr. Urban."

Grady pivoted and extended his hand for a shake. "Good to see you, Dr. Knox."

"Pete," he insisted, locking hands with Grady in a hearty greeting. "You remember my wife, Carla?"

Grady released his hand and extended it to Carla. "How do you do?"

The rail-thin woman returned a pharmaceutically enhanced smile but said nothing. Her hand was like trying to grip a piece of limp linguine. There was no warm satisfaction in the shared touch, and Grady wasn't even sure how many parts of this woman existed in their natural state.

She pulled back her hand and brushed a strand of over-processed hair from her cheek.

Her fingernails shone more brightly than glow-in-the-dark street reflectors. Above her eyes, a thick layer of eye shadow created a purple haze atop her lids that looked like heavy fog descending.

Women were beautiful in their natural state. Why they felt the need to sometimes alter that was a mystery to Grady.

"So how's Seguin treating you?" Dr. Knox asked.

"Good."

"That's a short answer."

Grady wasn't sure how much to reveal to Dr. Knox. Did he really want to hear about his slate of needy patients like Poppy McDougal or aberrant ones like Skylar, the cat-eye contact coveting teen and her text-happy mother? Was Grady being petty by wanting all patient interactions to go a certain way?

"And the practice itself?" Now came the prying questions Grady didn't want. "Are you getting any momentum?"

Grady shifted his weight. "I've managed to get things off the ground."

"It's just you as optometrist, right?" Dr. Knox worked at the hospital, so though he was asking about this specialty practice, Grady wasn't sure if he could truly relate.

"Just me. And three staff members."

"Yes. Sorry. I didn't mean to imply—"

"No worries."

"It's just that I'm used to the fast pace of the emergency room."

"I understand."

"Not every branch of medicine operates at such break-neck speed."

"Definitely not optometry. At least most days." That was one of the reasons Grady enjoyed the field.

"Are you finding enough clients?"

"A few new ones each week. I'm proud of that."

"Good, good." Dr. Knox assessed. "Lots of new clients are good."

He hadn't said lots of clients. This week, Grady could count the number on two hands, with the latest being Danica Lara. Her name and their two encounters were easy to recollect. Some mental images regarding patients weren't fresh in his mind. But with this woman, his memory was a different story.

"Keep up the good work." Dr. Knox raised his hand again and clapped it on Grady's shoulder in a fraternity-like clutch.

Grady thanked Dr. Knox for the show of support and as the two departed, extended his well wishes to Knox's wife for a pleasant rest of the evening. He was glad to know other doctors—and be in their company at this gala—but he also felt like a bit of an imposter still in an area where he had yet to fully gain his footing.

Turning from the scratchy encounter, Grady tugged at the collar of his shirt, took a deep breath, and steeled himself for more medical hobnobbing and posh small talk with other gala attendees. He didn't feel like he quite belonged, but if he was ever going to, he needed to at least act the part.

~*~

Danica told herself never to perform an Internet search on another acronym.

Ever.

She once did that when her younger cousin snickered at Danica for not knowing 4EAE. So she asked.

"For ever and ever." Teenage eyes must have rolled all around the globe that day.

"Got it." Danica had no idea under what circumstance she'd ever need to know that piece of information, so she stored it in some back drawer of her mental recesses.

"Do you know NTS?"

"No."

Her young cousin had been incredulous. "Note to self."

Danica played on the words with her own brand of humor. "I'll note that."

More eye rolling.

Decoding teen social media acronyms was not territory into which Danica cared to wade.

"SMH." Her cousin retorted.

Shaking my head.

Danica mimed the movement. Indeed.

So when Danica saw SES scrawled on the Friday square of her calendar, she immediately thought it must have been some acronym she knew at one time and then promptly forgot. To check, she did an Internet search.

If it actually was a texting abbreviation, she couldn't find it. An Internet shortcut was a possibility as well, though it wasn't clear. Links to supply equipment companies, municipal holdings, foreign sites, and even a girl band begged to be clicked, yet nothing Danica saw jarred her memory.

"I feel so old," Danica mumbled of her inability to decipher the letters, even with technology at her fingertips. She closed her laptop screen, looking back at her paper calendar. She set her finger atop the square as she thought, as if its pressure would cause the answer to reveal itself like a magician's best trick.

"This is ridiculous." Danica voiced her frustration aloud. "A kid should be able to figure this out."

And, *voila*, not unlike a performer taking stage, the illusion of the letters was revealed.

Seguin Elementary School.

Such a childish set of letters to forget. Danica's brain should have been sharper than it was, and in moments like this, she wondered about her own sanity. And, as she had mentioned to Paige, those pesky effects from age. Why, oh why, had she not appreciated the alertness and mental stamina she had in her twenties?

Danica flipped back open her laptop and initialized another search. Arriving at the Seguin Elementary School homepage, she clicked through the links to the academic calendar. The school year had just started, so weekly meetings would be kicking in for DEAR time.

Another acronym. Danica shook the frustration of words and their meanings shrinking before her.

This acronym, though, she remembered. Drop

Everything and Read was an elementary school literacy initiative to help students who needed a little bit of extra one-on-one attention. Reading problems were solved by intervention, and community volunteers helped to that end. Once a week, an adult volunteer was paired with a student who needed extra practice. Adults could read to kids, have kids read to them, play word association games, and boost a child's confidence in the process. It was a forty-minute obligation, and Danica was asked to fill in for another appraisal office volunteer who took maternity leave during what was the kids' last few weeks of school. Luckily, the office allowed a half day of paid volunteerism a month at an employee's discretion, so partnering with the school had been a great match. At the end of the year, the teacher in charge had asked Danica if she would like to volunteer for the upcoming academic year's pool.

Danica agreed, and here she was. A summer passed, a school year started, and a commitment already promised for the upcoming Friday.

~*~

The medical gala's jazz band kicked the post-dinner festivities into gear. Some decided to let loose on the dance floor, which was cleared in the middle of the hall. Others perused the corner space devoted to silent auction items. Small groups buzzed with conversation, and others mingled and socialized.

Grady stayed seated since he was finishing his

dessert of pecan pie. As he took a final bite, his tablemate to the right started to sway to the beat of the music. She was a widow of a past member of the board. Grady laid his fork across his dessert plate and dabbed the corner of his mouth with his cloth napkin. "Good music."

"I'll say." She didn't miss a beat. "Are you planning on cutting a rug out there, Dr. Urban?"

Grady shook his head. "Not if I can avoid it."

"Don't tell me you're not a dancer." The woman held one hand in the air and another across her chest as she sashayed from her seated position.

"Then I won't tell you." He smiled and folded his napkin.

The woman raised her chin higher in the air, miming a movement beneath an invisible partner's outstretched arm. She was completely lost in her own world of dancing from her chair. "So dancing's not in your blood?"

"Is that where the gene resides?" Grady could appreciate the balance and skill needed to move, but he had zero training when it came to learning to dance.

"It does in me." The woman beamed with a pride of dance appreciation years in the making.

Grady hoped she wasn't angling for a twirl around the floor. "I'm afraid you will have to find someone who has better genes than me."

"Oh honey," she swatted the air between them, "Your genes are fine as far as I can see. You've got it all. Blond hair like some storybook prince. Strong arms and hands." She lowered her voice as she added, "Not an inch of fat on you like some of the farm boys around here." She straightened her posture. "A real prize, if you ask me."

"Thank you." Grady knew little else to say to the elderly woman's compliments.

"And I'm not the only woman in the room who thinks so." The words overran Grady's flattery-focused thoughts as the widow directed his attention to the stare of a woman across the room.

Iris.

How Grady hadn't seen her before now was a surprise. True, there were hundreds of people at the gala, and maybe not all had bought tickets for the actual dinner. Perhaps some—Iris included?—had only arrived for the after-party.

"She can't take her eyes off you."

Iris cast a smile and delivered a dainty-fingered wave when she saw the two of them looking her direction. Grady returned a simple show of acknowledgement by raising his hand. At no point this week in the office had Iris mentioned attending the gala. "She's my assistant technician."

The widow smacked her lips in derision. "I bet she is."

Were all senior citizen women in this part of the state card-carrying sass-talkers?

"How long has she been looking over here?"

"She's been staring at you since she got here, honey." She leaned in for another private comment. "And, if you ask me, that tight dress is her way of sending a message."

Iris's youthful curves were hugged by a cocktail dress, the likes of which Grady had never seen on her. He knew Iris in boxy work scrubs. Here, satiny red fabric clung to her sides in a pleasing silhouette of shape. A v-cut neckline begged for attention, as did the mid-thigh hem of her skirt. Tanned and toned legs glided into stiletto heels, another first for Iris. "I've never seen her look like that."

"I think that's precisely the point." As if on cue, Iris pivoted like a runway model, cupped her hair into her hand, and gave it a primp. "That girl's got it bad for you."

Grady suddenly felt as if he were caught in some high school prom moment, a spooling scene that didn't match his age or the professional nature of this gala. True, everyone was dressed to the nines in formalwear, but voicing a compliment of Iris on such a sexy look didn't seem right.

Grady's thoughts tugged back to the scene in which he was caught.

"She looks like she wants to dance. Are you going to ask her?" the woman next to him prompted.

Not only did Grady have no skills in that arena, but sharing an intimate dance with Iris would send the wrong message. "No dance genes, remember?"

"Honey, it's not how you dance that matters. Sometimes a woman just wants to be close to a man."

And that was precisely the problem. He had committed to no work-related romances. And though Iris was a knockout tonight, he couldn't dare say so, nor could he make any move in the direction of her thinking the two of them had a chance at coupling.

Because they didn't.

She was his employee, and that's all the two of them could be. His sweetheart was his business, and he needed to keep it running smoothly before he could expect his personal life to operate at such a speed.

SIX

Danica used her Wednesday lunch to slip over to Spectacle Optique to try on frames. She entered the waiting room, but instead of checking in at the reception window with Samantha, she went straight to the wall with row upon row of frames that had appeared to be watching her the first time she stepped into the space.

Heath greeted her. "May I help you find something you like?"

"Maybe." Admittedly, Danica wasn't sure about what she wanted. "I have a prescription, so I need to pick some glasses."

"It is from Dr. Urban?"

"Yes."

"We take prescriptions from any optometrist. Some people like to come in and just shop for new frames or get a second set of glasses," Heath explained. "But I'm glad you used Dr. Urban's services. Is this your first pair?"

"Yes, so I have no idea what would even look good."

"I can help with that. And since you're a patient of Dr. Urban's, you'll get a 30% discount on anything you select."

That was a pleasant surprise.

Heath explained that the lenses and the frames were sold separately, a concept that was entirely new to Danica. "So the ones you're trying on today are just demos with non-magnifying lenses. A lab will prepare your custom lenses in whatever frames you choose, and then we can talk about anti-glare or scratch-resistant types. We even have some that dim in the sun."

After her experience with eye dilation, that sounded like a good idea.

"But first things first. Start with the frames," Heath directed. "Do you want to browse and pick a few that catch your attention, or would you like me to suggest some based on popularity?"

Danica scanned the countless options of styles. "I'll look around."

"Perfect." Heath pointed to the top of a vanity table with a pedestal mirror. "Stack what you like here, and then I can help adjust the frames to fit your face. Measuring will be the last thing we do."

Such a process to getting glasses. At least there was someone here to help. "Thank you."

"My pleasure." Heath advised her to ask if she needed anything. "Otherwise, just enjoy browsing."

The no-watching approach was just what she needed. Danica found a first pair with skinny, amber colored frames. She plucked them from their display, felt their weight, and tried them. They felt...there. Her ears, nose, and eyebrows all told her she was wearing glasses, a sensation she had only experienced with sunglasses. And that was entirely different. She checked her reflection in the mirror.

Not bad, style wise. But the tonal contrast wasn't right against her dark hair. She tried again, this time selecting black frames.

Cute, but not for her.

Danica continued the trial and error of choosing different shapes and frame colors until she settled on four that she thought looked good and whose weight was tolerable. Tiny triple-digit stickers in the upper right-hand corner prompted Danica to ask when Heath returned, "Is this a style number?"

"That's the price," he corrected.

Gulp.

Those digits were a little rich for Danica's blood, considering there was the cost of the lenses yet to consider. And the glasses' carrying case. "Or does that come with the frames?"

"That's complimentary."

A small victory.

"Remember, you get a discount. And glasses will be a permanent part of how people see you. So you want frames that you feel are right."

"I want frames that don't sink my paycheck."

"We've got some that don't do that." Heath didn't sugarcoat the reality as he picked up each of Danica's selections one by one. "But you did pick some of the most expensive frames we carry. You have stylish tastes."

Danica groaned, but before she could answer, another voice added to the conversation. "I knew you had style." Dr. Urban appeared behind her, his reflection catching first in the mirror before Danica spun to face him.

"Hello." His white doctor's coat was unfastened all the way down, revealing a pair of pressed khakis and a coral-colored polo shirt that stretched tight across his chest. The summery colors combined with his blond hair and his black-framed glasses made him look model perfect.

"Glad you came back in for these." He dug one hand casually into his pants pocket, opening his coat farther and showing off a physique that Danica thought was a shame to hide. "Are you finding some you like?"

She gestured to the four frames she was considering. "Maybe."

"Danica has some great options. Want to sit down and try them on?" Heath pulled out the vanity stool for customer use. "Let's have a look at all of them."

"Yes." Dr. Urban dug his other hand into his side pocket, a cool move toward settling in to watch. "Let's have a look."

Single, Danica Lara had now captured the attention of two men. And did she have any choice in disappointing them? She accepted the stool, slid into place next to the mirror with her back toward the men, and shook her hair back from her shoulders in preparation to try on the first pair.

"Pair number one," Danica held up oval tortoise shell frames with brushed bronze finishing. She placed them on, turning slightly right and left to judge their appropriateness before asking her surprise audience, "What do you think?"

"A great first choice," Heath said.

But it was Dr. Urban to whom Danica slid her gaze in a sly move, wondering most what he thought. His reflection in the mirror showed a cocked head of serious consideration.

"I'm going to disagree."

Danica's eyes widened behind the lenses.

"The pattern detracts too much from your face. And nothing needs to compete with that."

Was that flattery? Danica's stomach did a quick somersault. "OK," she managed, willing herself to stay calm. "Shall I try the next pair?"

Dr. Urban didn't make a move to go anywhere.

She tried the next two pairs. One was an invisible frame with lens held together by thin titanium parts, and the other one was a full-rim wood textured frame. "These are about as different as can be." She tried one and then the other—then went back to the invisible frames. "These are kind of neat." She turned her head to one side before asking her audience, "What do you think?"

Heath offered a generic compliment that didn't influence Danica one way or another. But when Dr. Urban spoke his opinion, it did. "That's the best one so far for showing off those sparklers." Maybe it was because that fun name for her eyes was like a pet name for her, and even if he said it to all of his clients, hearing it directed at her made Danica shine on the outside and inside.

"I have one more." She pinched the last set of frames between her thumb and forefinger, still a bit surprised she grabbed them in the first place. Danica didn't originally think turquoise frames would be a style she liked, but when she first put them on, the color popped against her espresso-colored hair, even making the brown color of her eyes look striking. She set the frames into place, squared her shoulders, and raised her head for the reveal.

Heath expressed approval with a "looks really good" comment, but Dr. Urban upped the compliment factor once again. "Those were made for you." He smiled a broad, approving smile that broke the veneer of professional courtesy and ventured into territory more personal, especially when he added "beautiful" as a final assessment when Danica met his gaze in the mirror. Locking gazes, Danica wasn't sure if the sexy superhero alter-ego of a doctor at her back was just referring to the glasses—or if he were referring to her.

"Heath, can we do any better than a 30% discount on those?" Dr. Urban kept his eyes on Danica. "I don't want these frames to have any reason not to be worn by Miss Lara."

Heath agreed to cut the price an extra 20%. "Boss's orders," he winked.

Danica pushed the glasses atop her head, her bangs feathering back from the smooth frames that now acted like a headband. "I'll take them!"

"A wonderful choice," Heath said. "Now, if you'll excuse me, I need to get an order form from the back."

That left Danica and Dr. Urban alone. There

wasn't even another patient in the waiting room side of the space the whole time she was shopping for frames.

"A lull in business?" she inquired.

He shrugged casually. "Just consider this personalized service."

"You're quite good at that," The words leapt from Danica's mouth before she could consider how they sounded. Too coy? Too flirty?

"It's easy with you." Dr. Urban's response was so simple, yet the weight of the words hit Danica hard.

Now that's flirty.

Like a foot massage in a pedicure chair where fingers hit all the right spots, Dr. Urban was doing the same with his words. They affected her all the way from toes to those eyes at which he couldn't stop staring.

And neither could Danica.

True, he was an optometrist, yet the way he looked at her bore more deeply than a patient-doctor relationship. Surely, he didn't do that with all of his patients.

Right?

She was the first to avert her gaze, reaching her hand to remove the frames before tucking loose strands of hair behind both ears. She cleared her throat of rising nerves before trying to speak. But as she made the move to do so, Heath returned with his paperwork, launching right back into business mode with an overview of the eyeglass ordering process.

"Guess that's my cue to jet," Dr. Urban interjected.

Heath looked up. "Were you on your way out?"

"Just briefly." Dr. Urban slipped both arms out of his coat, stowing it over his arm—like a superhero revealing his true identity. Danica was able to see yet another layer to the doctor as he stood without his uniform. She still liked absolutely everything she saw.

And she wasn't the only one.

The corner of the mirror caught a second surprise reflection, a woman's head peeking around the hallway entrance by reception. Even without glasses, there was no mistaking the blonde locks and nosey intrusion of Iris.

"I'm on my way to the school," Dr. Urban continued. "I have to sign some paperwork for the reading program before I start working with the kids."

Danica's ears perked at the mention. SES? She wanted to ask. The third grade group? But what were the chances he was volunteering in the same way as she was? Danica didn't have an opportunity to clarify as Dr. Urban waved his good-byes and stepped toward the exit. He left her with a parting comment of "nice decision again on the glasses" as well as a soft touch on the shoulder before parting ways.

Iris's head disappeared from view just as Dr. Urban slid from Danica's. Alone with Heath, she tried to focus on the task at hand. Yet all she could feel was the lingering sensation of Dr. Urban's hand atop her shoulder, a quiet gesture of contact that left Danica with emotions she couldn't pin down, even though she wanted to try.

"Do you have a preference of lenses?" Heath's question snapped her task squarely into focus again as he enumerated the choices. Yet even as she finished her decision for the eyewear she came to buy, she was concerned with another decision: what to do with these corporeal sensations that should not have been a part of an optical visit.

~*~

Danica saw Paige over the lunch hour on Thursday, a quick sack lunch they each brought to Walnut Springs Park and shared on a pedestrian trail bench that overlooked the emerald-colored springs that fed into the town's Guadalupe River.

"Are we getting old?" Danica inquired, taking in their surroundings. "We're like two old ladies, packing homemade sandwiches and sitting in a public park watching the water go by."

"Speak for yourself." Paige took pride in showing off her chic lunch bag as well as the contents inside: a sport bottle of strawberry infused water, a sprout and avocado sandwich, and a bag of organic quinoa chips. "And I've got these dark chocolate covered espresso beans that are absolutely divine." She held up a tiny pouch.

"Looks like someone is giving lunch an overhaul." Danica pulled out her contents.

"And looks like someone else needs to do the same." Paige pointed to Danica's paltry choices. "You could jazz up those sides."

"Don't knock my string cheese." Danica waved the wand of floppy mozzarella in cartoon-themed packaging.

"Just wondering if you have a thermos of decaf in there too that you're going to pour into a plastic mug and then—"

"I have cranberry juice, thank you very much." Danica tapped the name brand plastic bottle.

"Oh," Paige rolled her eyes. "That's not old-ladyish in the least."

"Eat your sprouts."

The friends ate in silence for a few moments before Paige asked, "Do you really feel old?"

"I think we have this conversation routinely." She took a bite of her sandwich.

"I know." Paige hemmed and hawed her words. "But I'm just wondering if, well, you feel…"

Danica swallowed her bite. "Spit it out."

"Do you feel different than you did in your twenties?"

"Absolutely." No contest there.

"How?" Paige asked.

Those answers were easy ones. "More confident. Less edgy. Not as much worry about the little things." Not that her twenty-something years weren't fun. "Thirty is just…" She searched for the word.

"More settled?" Paige offered.

Danica weighed that last word. "Sort of."

"Even without—"

"Don't say it." Danica knew what Paige was going to ask before she even asked it. "I know I don't have a man."

"Not that you need one." Paige tried to dismiss

her faux pas.

Occasionally, Paige offered a romantic setup for her friend. She would mention someone she knew was single, an acquaintance of Everett's, or some other friend of a friend. Danica had been on her share of blind dates and double dates, some organic and some forced. No one—recently, at least—had stuck.

"At the Land & Title office," she led into the suggestion first with a casual mention. "Miguel's cousin came by. He lives in San Antonio."

Danica held up her free hand. "Is this a setup?"

Paige acted nonchalant. "If you want it to be."

Danica knew how Paige operated, so she let her continue.

"You know what a good boss Miguel is."

"Not from personal experience," Danica corrected.

"Right. But you know what a good person he's been to me." And Danica did. Through Paige's divorce and Nathan's medical needs when he was hospitalized for appendicitis a couple of years ago, Paige's office family had been incredibly supportive and responsive to the things she needed. And that could have happened only under the direction of office leadership that made everyone comfortable. Danica was glad the atmosphere at Paige's title office was the way it was.

She nodded understanding of her best friend's experience. "I've always liked Miguel."

"Then you'll really like his cousin."

"I walked right into that one, didn't I?" Maybe Danica needed to be more guarded with her singledom status.

Paige launched into the merits of this man that now Danica knew only by name. She listened in the same manner she had listened to advice from her mother: she took it with a grain of salt.

She could recall past adages that her mother recited as if she were hearing them in the present. "Brush your hair one hundred times before you go to bed," her mother routinely instructed when Danica was a teen. But running a brush through her strands ten times or one hundred times didn't seem to make a difference. Every morning when she awoke, her hair had managed to tangle itself.

"Did you brush your hair one hundred times last night?" her mom would ask upon seeing Danica struggling in the bathroom mirror to smooth her look before school. Her mother-knows-best question was one Danica ignored. Either way, her hair tangled.

She tried to explain that.

And it didn't matter to her mother.

From that experience, Danica had learned that some advice was best deflected rather than absorbed. So when Paige finished her sales pitch of this mystery man who was available for a setup, she asked Danica what she thought.

Danica drew from her well of experience in dealing with advice from her mother. She nodded in polite acknowledgement, thanked her friend, and gave a noncommittal "I'll think about it."

"You will?" Paige's enthusiasm showed she completely missed the mark of Danica's response.

"I'll let you know." Danica stayed vague.

"I won't mention anything to Miguel just yet." Paige apparently remained blind to Danica's disinterest.

Now Danica needed clarity on how far along this matchmaking had already gone. "You've asked him?"

"No," Paige explained. "But I did meet his cousin last week, and I think he'd be worth a shot."

Now those words weren't exactly a glowing recommendation.

Such was the reality of setups, especially since she was no longer interested in meeting men in forced social settings or through any sort of digital-media-type service. Dates needed to be organic, and so did the connections themselves.

Danica wanted easy.

Unexpected.

She wanted an allure that was natural, not forced.

Butterflies in her stomach. Stars in her eyes. And her heart in her throat. She wanted to feel like…

Like she did when Dr. Urban was around.

She nailed the type of experience she wanted. What came as the greatest surprise, though, was how Dr. Urban himself had nailed it.

So was he a romantic possibility? Or was he just being an attentive doctor whose cues she misread because that's what she wanted to see in him?

SEVEN

Grady might as well have been a giant among the lines of children who marched the third-grade hallway at Seguin Elementary on their way to the school cafeteria.

"Bubbles and tails!" one teacher commanded from the front of the lines. A ripple effect of children smacked their lips closed with chipmunk cheeks full of air, quieting the space.

Aaah, Grady reasoned. The bubbles.

Next, the children locked their hands behind their backs, lock-stepping their way in controlled single file to the cafeteria.

That move must be the tails.

Grady was impressed by the control. He remembered his public school cafeteria days characterized by much more noise and chaos. And that, like this scene, was before he and his classmates stepped foot into the actual lunch lines.

Grady slowed his own speed as he passed the children like a salmon swimming upstream. Each set of eyes studied him in turn as he passed child after child. Some clutched colorful lunch boxes or patterned sacks. Varying heights with some students a head taller than the rest showed pediatric growth in action.

And all those eyes…

The parade of youthful vision made him wonder how many of these kiddos he might see in the years to come. He hoped many would use the services of Spectacle Optique, if, indeed, they needed a checkup, a diagnosis, or a referral. Creating a pipeline within the community was the idea in starting the business, and keeping it going could only happen with a public presence and community involvement.

Which is why when a representative from the DEAR program at SES contacted Grady to ask if his new business might be interested in a once-a-week involvement with third grade students, he'd said "Yes."

He paused at the open door to Mrs. Livingston's classroom, knocking against the jamb to announce his presence.

She looked up from her desk, greeting him with all the enthusiasm he expected from an elementary teacher. "You must be Dr. Urban!"

He nodded, stepping inside the door and extending his hand as she rose to meet him halfway. "You can call me Grady."

"It's such a pleasure to meet you." She shook his hand as enthusiastically as a long-lost aunt, her skin lotion-soft in an aged way. "Do come in. Do come in." She tried to make him feel as at home as if this were his own.

And knowing how hard teachers worked, he suspected she probably spent as much time here as she did at her own residence.

"Thank you for meeting with me today to go over the program."

"I should be the one thanking you." She brought her hand to her chest in a gesture of complete gratitude. "These kiddos are so special to me, and this program is an absolute joy to run." Sincerity shone through her enthusiasm, even though Grady sensed in her words that she might be a teacher fatigued by her own level of passion for education. "But it can't happen without volunteers."

"I'm happy to be a part of it." Grady hoped the words weren't premature, considering he actually knew very little about the content of the program.

"You're a doll for answering my call and agreeing to participate." She motioned toward a chair at the nearest table. "Would you like to have a seat?"

"Sure thing." He sat in a comfortable yet simple plastic chair next to one the same color but which was built for a body half the size of his own. There were about a dozen tables like that in the room, each paired with two chairs: one big, one small.

As if noticing what Grady was seeing for the first time, Mrs. Livingston offered an explanation. "This is how we sit. One community volunteer per table next to the assigned student. We feel it's best for a student to have a side-by-side interaction to create more of a mentorship than sitting across from them at a table."

Grady understood the rationale now that she explained it. "I see."

"When you sit shoulder to shoulder with a child, it's easy to turn the pages of a book, participate together in the experience, and not make the student feel like he or she is on display."

"Do the same children come in all year?"

"Yes, you'll follow the same student week to week. I've got you paired with a little girl named Alexis. Cute as a button, she is. A real sweet kid who's a little shy, but I bet she'll warm up once she meets you."

Grady wondered if Alexis was one of the children whom he had already passed in the hallway as the children walked to lunch. There was no way to know, but if she had already seen him, perhaps the sight of a grown man next to her in a reading classroom for forty minutes on a Friday wouldn't be as great of a shock. "About that." He did have one thing to ask.

"Yes?"

"I plan to be here this Friday. But, as you mentioned, I spoke with my staff, and the four of us are agreeable to rotating week to week."

"I see." Mrs. Livingston couldn't conceal the crestfallen look that washed in reaction to Grady's words.

A pin drop could have exploded the pregnant silence. "Did I misunderstand the options for volunteering?" Grady had figured once-a-month visits shuffled between Iris, Samantha, Heath, and he made the most sense to the running of their office. For such a short time, each could cover another in absence, and he would tell Samantha simply not to schedule optical exams for the Friday morning time once a month when he would be the designated volunteer.

"No, you didn't misunderstand." Sitting face-to-face perhaps allowed more honesty than their previous conversation simply over the phone. "You can absolutely do that, if you like. And we are so, so grateful," she added quickly.

Grady sensed there was more.

"But if there's any way for a stable commitment for one-on-one mentorship, that's what I advise. SES tries to give these students as much stability as possible when it comes to routine." Mrs. Livingston stressed how these students who were identified for individualized literacy attention didn't get the development they needed at home. "For a variety of reasons," she breezed, careful perhaps to protect student privacy. "So if we are able to develop a routine with the same mentor week to week, we see much greater success with students."

Grady hadn't thought of the reasons behind why each student was enrolled in the program. He especially hadn't considered home factors, but now that he did, his heart tugged at situations he didn't know but suspected Mrs. Livingston did. If they were enough to inform her running of the program in this way, he would do what he could to meet the needs she saw. "I can come this Friday—"

"Wonderful!" she sang her praise of happy gratitude once again.

Although Grady was hesitant to overcommit, he said he'd arrive the Friday after that as well. "And then how about I play it by ear after that?"

Mrs. Livingston clasped her hands in contented triumph. "Absolutely. Dr. Urban, I couldn't ask for any more. Thank you for answering the call to volunteer, and thank you for helping Seguin Elementary."

"I'm glad to do so." Truly, Grady was. He wasn't seeking a role like this, but, reflecting on his own experience learning to read, a literacy mentorship was a small commitment that he suspected would yield big personal rewards.

As if understanding Grady's thought process, Mrs. Livingston hammered home a final pitch for the program. "Most of our volunteers say they get more from their experience than the kiddos."

"Is that right?"

"The results might surprise you." Mrs. Livingston gave a knowing smile.

Grady would have to wait and see about that.

~*~

Friday morning Danica dressed in a two-toned wrap dress that was as comfortable to wear as it was to accessorize.

All she really needed was shoes.

Dresses, she had learned from Paige, could be a woman's best wardrobe secret. Wearing them didn't require coordination between a top and bottom. Depending on the footwear, they could be dressed up or dressed down. They always made a feminine statement. And the best part was the fabric: she bought only low-wrinkle, no-iron material that was machine-washable. When Paige suggested as much, Danica thought options would be extremely limited.

"Not if you know where to look!"

Over the years, Paige had happily advised of her favorite brands and stores until Danica found the rhythm of discovering her own. Paige's sister, Mallory, also helped indirectly. That girl had the jewelry sense of an artisan, so Danica got style ideas from Mallory every time she visited the area or whenever Paige received a photo or text from her sister. Danica credited Mallory with teaching her that long necklaces in layers, stackable rings, and dangly earrings could be worn all together or one piece at a time to make an eye-catching statement.

Today, Danica's dress was beige and black, classic color blocking in a modern style that stood out on its own. If she'd had her turquoise glasses, they really would have popped against the fabric. Too bad she had to wait a week for them to be made. Two days after placing the order—and seeing the look on Dr. Urban's face before she did—she was excited by the choice and ready to embrace a life with chic frames.

She turned right to left, judging the look in the full-length mirror. "That's the right amount of color," she assessed. Now, not wanting anything to compete with the statement necklace, she simply added some basic leather ballet flats and a set of small sterling silver hoops. "Perfection."

She stopped by the office for an hour, answering e-mails and setting the day's priorities in order before traveling to the SES campus. As she had been told to do, she parked in a visitor's spot, entered through the door closest to the main office, and checked in for school safety clearance. She knew Mrs. Livingston's room was but a short walk one building away from the office.

Scents of elementary school craft activities—glue, playdough, markers—mingled with the kiddos responsible for the budding artistry behind closed classroom doors. Kitschy classroom welcome signs and seasonal art decorated doors as Danica stepped past one by one on her way to Mrs. Livingston's.

And that classroom scent was as she remembered.

Books. Photocopies. And spiral notebooks.

Anyone who thinks paper doesn't have a distinct smell had never stepped foot in Mrs. Livingston's classroom. Something about all of those words, pages, and blank paper possibilities made it a veritable joy to sniff.

But as Danica turned the corner into the room, she saw a face she didn't expect in the least.

"Dr. Urban?" The superhero alter-ego of a doctor had shed his white lab coat monogrammed with his name for an adhesive school name badge instead.

Which was not a bad look for him. As much as she liked a man in uniform—any uniform would do—street clothes on superhero handsome Grady Urban were so much better.

He blinked behind his hipster glasses before greeting her with a broad smile and a wave to come closer. As she followed his lead, his soap-clean scent breezed toward her.

And as much as she liked the smell of books and paper, his distinct, sexy smell was so much better.

"What are you doing here?" she asked of him, this surprise doctor among third graders.

"Playing hooky from work," he winked.

"You?" Danica couldn't hide her skepticism, for even she sensed from her visits how seriously he handled his practice. "Doubtful."

"You caught me," he teased further. "Send me to the principal." This playful side of the doctor was a personality reversal she didn't expect. Maybe being in a classroom just brought out the kid in him.

"You better not get in trouble here." She added, "Or at your office." She thought about Heath, Samantha, and Iris. "Can that place operate without a doctor?"

"They'll manage for forty minutes," he assured her, sporting every bit of cool confidence. "And, please, you don't have to refer to me as the doc here." He lowered his voice, speaking exclusively to her. "Just calling me Grady is fine."

Now she was on a first name basis with the good doctor.

And that was all right by her.

"Just calling me Danica is fine too," she offered in kind.

"I remembered your name."

"I'm sure you did." She gestured toward her temple, tapping the spot in recollection of her inaugural encounter with him.

"How's your forehead feeling, by the way?" He mimed for her to brush her bangs to the side so that he could peek.

"You be the judge." Danica had felt fine for days. The swelling dissipated over the weekend, and even when she was trying on frames two days ago, sliding them off and on didn't present any problem.

"Beautiful." Every analysis by him—in office and out—solicited a sensation just like flattery. Was that because it was? Or was that just Danica's wishful thinking on overdrive?

Grady shifted to another focus. "You don't have your glasses on yet."

"I was told by Heath they would come in next week."

Grady nodded. "I'm sure he'll give you a call as soon as they arrive."

"I'm actually excited to get them." The level of childlike eagerness that came with each passing day simply put her one step closer toward those frames that she knew would make a difference in her daily encounters. But their colorful, unique look made her eager for their accessorizing potential too.

"You should be." He tapped the corner of his own. "And I think it's good for kids to see adults in glasses, especially for reading." Turning his attention toward the task at the school that brought them together, he explained how many kids had an aversion to glasses. Embarrassment and stereotype caused some children to have an ill-understanding of them, until, as Grady explained, "they see someone they know wearing them. They can ask questions and feel comfortable. That goes a long way."

Danica agreed. She was here to help, and maybe

she'd even be paired with a kid who wore glasses. That would, now that she considered it, be a neat connection for them both. "Now, if you'll excuse me, I need to let Mrs. Livingston know I'm here."

"By all means." Grady gave a slight head nod as Danica stepped back from the conversation and made her way to Mrs. Livingston, who was introducing the process to two new volunteers who had arrived.

Seeing Danica, Mrs. Livingston extended her arms for a mamma bear welcome. "So good to see you! Thank you for coming back this year."

"I couldn't turn you down." That was a fact. Mrs. Livingston might be a mother hen of the school children over whose care she was entrusted in the classroom, but she was a pit bull when it came to the one-on-one needs of the children who were a part of the DEAR program. Even in the short time Danica helped the previous school year, she knew Mrs. Livingston had a special place in her heart for these kids as well as the means to reach them.

"Any quick questions?" Mrs. Livingston asked.

"Just one." A kid with glasses was a very small thing, but Grady had planted in her head that it may be a way to immediately connect. "I just wanted to ask you if the kids have already been assigned to the volunteers."

"Yes." Why would Danica have thought the answer would be any different, knowing this teacher's level of preparation? "I have the names over there, and the kids will be arriving any minute. In fact, it's time to get ready." She clapped her hands three times to get everyone's attention, commanding the classroom regardless of the ages of those who sat in its seats. "Welcome, thank you, and let's take our places to get ready for our DEAR kids!"

Mrs. Livingston placed her hand on Danica's back, ushering her along to the nearest available seat at the table unoccupied.

Front and center.

And, with a schoolgirl level of surprise, Danica couldn't have been more tickled that the table was next to the hot doctor she considered to be the cutest boy in the room.

EIGHT

Mrs. Livingston directed each student to a predetermined table with their mentor. "Remember to introduce yourself, and then answer your list of favorites." A worksheet split into two columns with questions like What's your favorite color? and What's your favorite animal? cut down the page, with space for the student and the mentor each to write answers. It was a clever icebreaker, something age-appropriate and easy for a first meeting.

Danica watched child after child parade past until one lone boy with a mop top of hair and a tender looking scar cut diagonally across his forehead, made his way to the seat next to her. "Hi," she mustered her most personable voice. "I'm Danica."

"Owen," he averted his gaze, keeping his head low. The bright-eyed enthusiasm she expected was nowhere in sight.

A clattering of voices rose around them, duos in happy conversation with cheery intonations. "I'm here to get to know you. I'm glad you came to Mrs. Livingston's room."

"I was told to come to this room," Owen muttered.

So this was how the experience was going to start. Danica took a deep breath, doing her best to continue her cheerfulness in spite of the boy's less than earnest response. "Shall we try these questions?"

Owen hunched his shoulders.

No reply.

Danica slid a pencil to him.

No reaction.

Danica asked if Owen wanted her to go first with writing her answers.

No movement.

Disinterest was an understatement.

Danica had encountered plenty of crotchety, fussy taxpayers during her years at the appraisal district. Especially during appeal hearings, some of the hardest sessions to sit through were those where the person across the table was defiant or virtually non-responsive. Each person required a different level of handling. Sometimes one approach worked, sometimes another.

Occasionally, nothing worked.

Danica would do everything in her power to not make today one of those days. She took another breath before diving back into an attempt to crack Owen's shell.

She grasped her pencil between her fingers, angled the worksheet near to her, and started to draw a picture in the box next to the animal question.

Danica was no artist. So this was a stretch.

But it was her best idea.

She kept an eye on Owen in her periphery as she drew in silence, seeing him lift his head upward with interest the longer she stayed silent and drew. After more than a minute of drawing, he still hadn't said a word, so Danica asked without looking up from the page, "Do you know what a liger is?"

Owen didn't answer with words or a gesture, but he also didn't try to run away.

Progress.

Danica stayed the course.

"It's a cross between a tiger and a lion." She added a long tail to her drawing. "Two of the fiercest beasts in the animal kingdom." She pretended to be completely absorbed in her small drawing, all the while keeping an eye on Owen without his knowing.

Danica added teeth and a mane before she asked Owen if she should draw stripes or spots. "Or both, since it's a liger? What do you think?"

"Spots." His answer was barely above a whisper.

Now we're getting somewhere. Her anxiety level dropped several degrees. "Good choice." She dotted with the edge of her pencil tip in teeny, controlled circles.

All around them, murmurs continued as she caught pieces of conversation about favorite things. She was taking an unconventional approach, but it proved to work when Owen piped up with a question of his own. "Aren't you supposed to just write an answer?"

Danica flashed comical surprise and brought her hand to her mouth to snicker a cartoonish laugh. "We could," she paused for dramatic effect, "but drawing is so much more fun, don't you think?"

Owen flashed the faintest hint of a smile as he

nodded. His forehead scar bent like a lightning bolt as he moved, and Danica felt simultaneously sorry and concerned for whatever had caused that. But she wasn't going to ask. Today was all about first impressions and getting comfortable.

Just make progress.

She put the finishing touches on her liger before moving the paper in front of Owen. "Are you ready to draw your favorite animal?" She prompted in her most gentle voice.

Owen reached into the deep pockets of athletic shorts that looked two sizes too big on him, pulled out something that slid into his hand, which Danica couldn't fully see, and turned his head away from her.

When he turned back, his eyes were framed by sporty red glasses. He adjusted their fit on his nose, bent his head, and drew with an abandon of interest that was a complete one-hundred eighty-degree turn from the moments before.

Danica couldn't wait to see Owen's drawing. And she couldn't wait to show him her own glasses next week during their second DEAR time meeting. She was going to connect with this kid, one way or another.

~*~

Forty minutes passed in record speed for Grady. Alexis, his paired third grader, was exactly as Mrs. Livingston had said she would be. Cute as a button, a bit shy, but such a joy. Her two front teeth were missing, so she had an adorable temporary lisp when she sounded out words and letters. She was focused, too. Grady could tell by the concentration she gave as she put her finger beneath letter sets and sounded out syllables in words she read aloud. Grady wasn't sure of the exact role he should take, so he let her set the pace in answering their worksheet questions.

"This is fun!" he admitted to Alexis. Answering questions about favorite foods, pets, weather, and more were all meaningful to a third grader, but he found a simple joy in responding to them as well. Alexis, to her credit, was a trouper.

"You'll have to tell me what that is." He pointed to her answer for favorite cartoon show with a title he didn't recognize. Or maybe it was misspelled.

Even if it was, Alexis launched into a frenzied explanation of this animated fantasy world that was an entirely new subject to hear about for Grady. He didn't have to share her enthusiasm to appreciate it.

Several times, out of the corner of his eye, he caught Danica and the boy with whom she was paired. They sat close, but if they were talking, he saw no indication of it. No shoulder movements with laughter, no gestures with their hands, no shifting with interest in the chair from banter back and forth.

He hoped she was doing OK. Maybe her approach was just different. Or maybe her assigned student was.

Grady directed his attention back to Alexis. This petite girl had big potential.

They finished their worksheet, discussed their answers, and then both raised their hands as Mrs. Livingston had instructed so she could be called over for the next and only other step in their short DEAR-time curriculum. "How did it go?" she asked, directing her attention more at Alexis than Grady.

Alexis smiled a seemingly contented, front toothless smile at Mrs. Livingston, who took the obvious cue before she looked over the worksheet, mentally read through the answers, and told Alexis she had a book specifically for her based on her list of favorite things. She came back with a hardback book that had drawings of horses on the front. "Because you said you like ponies," she said as she handed the book to Alexis. "And when you're ready, give it to Dr. Urban because he is going to read it to you."

Alexis wasted no time, practically shoving the book into Grady's hands in anticipation for the story to begin.

He was raising his hand in a classroom.

He was reading a storybook about ponies.

And though these were reasons enough to feel like a kid, there was one more. He was stealing glances at a nearby female in the room, a certain Danica Lara who seemed to capture his attention no matter where he saw her.

"Are you a real doctor?" Alexis looked up at Grady as he turned open the first page of the book.

"Yes, I'm a real doctor," he affirmed with a bit of laughter.

"Do you help people?" Alexis pulled in the reigns of her eagerness for the pony story to ask about Grady. To be put before ponies: what a treat!

"I do try to help people."

Alexis chewed on those words. Children had such varying experience with doctors that he didn't dare ask about her perception of them here. But Alexis's curiosity toward him piqued his own about her. Did she want to be a doctor when she grew up? Did she have one in her family? Grady was already asking questions of interest he didn't think he would entertain on a first meeting with a third-grader. Starting with Alexis's eager grin, continuing with the worksheet questions, and ending with a conversation that she began made Grady realize the fun in this one-on-one program.

They only had ten minutes remaining, a perfect window for ponies. Grady read, Alexis listened, and both seemed to enjoy the simple beauty of a story unfolding page by page.

By the time Grady read the last page, he was a bit sad for the story to end. Forty minutes had flown by quickly. Mrs. Livingston thanked all the volunteers, told students to do the same, and then had them all line up for walking back to their homeroom class.

Alexis gave a quick-syllabled "bye" to Grady as she scurried to the front of the room to join the line. Grady noticed Danica's student also hurried, but in the gangly way that characterized many boys whose physical bodies developed more quickly than their social maturity.

Once the children left and the door closed behind them, Mrs. Livingston clasped her hands and delivered words of deep appreciation, making sure she included educational buzzwords like "engaging" and "affirming" and "mindful." Whether she believed those things or the talking points were part of a practiced speech that she might make to them each week remained to be seen. She did end with "You are all DEARs to me!" and chuckled jovially at her pun.

Grady pushed back his chair and stood, mirroring Danica as he did. "Thus ends our first week."

She bit her bottom lip as she pushed in her chair. "One down," she counted.

Grady was on a bit of a high from such an unexpectedly fun experience, but he wasn't sure if Danica's was the same. He wanted to debrief with her and ask about future visits since she mentioned that this was her second year of volunteering.

"Not second year, per se," she corrected. "I substituted for another mentor at the end of last year. It was fun, but I realized today how different that was. I was just filling in. So I missed all this first-of-the-year business." She waved her hand to swat the air as if the last word she spoke produced a fog.

Grady sensed frustration. "Is it more challenging because of that?"

She didn't answer, the non-response an answer in itself.

"Don't be hard on yourself," he coached, trying to sound caring and not cliché. He really didn't want Danica to take a rocky first start as an indicator of what was to come. "I expected as much myself, if that helps."

Danica slung her purse over her shoulder, still not saying a word.

Maybe it didn't. But Grady gave it one more shot. "It's only the first day."

Danica pivoted in an about-face to Grady. "Those," she pointed to his glasses. "I think I've got a way to connect to this kid with those."

Grady tried to keep his eyes from growing cross with Danica's finger in such close proximity to his nose. The pad of her finger swirled in a woozy pattern before him. His vision channeled a rigid fingerprint otherwise naked to most other eyes. The angle of her finger was set toward his glasses. "These?"

"Those." She avowed the word with the confidence of a knight on a quest. "I think he's nervous about wearing glasses. And next week when I get mine, I'll be able to show him they're not so bad, that lots of people wear them."

"Right," Grady reasoned, impressed by the admirable approach Danica was making toward finding some common ground with this boy. "Just like me."

Danica withdrew her finger and placed it against her chest to point at herself. "Just like us."

Us.

The collective word rang in Grady's ears. How long had it been since any woman included him with that word, involving him in a partnership? Not that there was a true partnership with Danica—who was he kidding?—but the word struck him nonetheless.

He wanted Danica to get her glasses.

He wanted them both to make a difference as literacy mentors.

But as he pushed back his sleeve to check the time, he also wanted to make sure his reality of running a business succeeded. He needed to get back to the office. He was sure Danica did, too.

They were professionals, after all. Time clocks to punch, responsibilities to meet, clients to service. This was how he saw them operating. Him going one way, her going another.

As much as it was fun to consider for a brief moment, there was no "us."

There was Grady.

There was Danica.

There were plenty of other men and women who existed in the singular, not the plural. That's just the space where he belonged for now.

NINE

Danica cupped her hand over the receiver of the telephone, keeping her voice low as she reprimanded Barry for calling her on the appraisal district office line.

"Did it ever occur to you that I am at work?" she hissed.

"That's why I called." Barry was not fazed.

"Use my cell phone," she scolded.

"You didn't pick up."

"Because I was busy." That, in itself, should have sent a message.

"But I needed to talk to you."

For the love of…sometimes, having a conversation with Barry Van Soyt was like speaking with a child. "What?" she seethed. "What is so important that it couldn't wait until I saw the missed call and returned it later?"

"Trees."

He had to be kidding. "Trees?"

"The contractor wants to knock out the pecan tree grove at the front of the property—"

"Hold it." Danica spoke as if the very moments themselves during this phone call determined the future of Cinnamon Ridge Estates. "No way. That's not in the cards. The plan was—"

"I know exactly what the plan was. I'm staring right at it." Paper crinkled on the other end of the line, but Danica didn't need her copy of the survey to know the exact grouping of trees to which Barry was referring. Mature trees incorporated in various lots and beautifying the entrance to the planned subdivision was one of their biggest selling points, something that set their development apart from every cookie-cutter contractor who plowed through nature, squared its offerings and sold lots with no regard for the land itself. That wasn't their approach.

Or maybe Danica should speak only for herself since Barry seemed to be wavering on their original agreement for the layout. "Those trees are not going anywhere. Period."

"That's not what the contractor said."

This conversation would have been so much easier if it weren't over the phone of her office line, coworkers passing by her cubicle and her work e-mail account pinging every few moments with new messages. She had to keep her voice in check as well as her professionalism.

"Is he there now?"

"Not with me."

She didn't know the location from which Barry was calling. That was the least of her worries. Their development plan was imploding faster than a helium balloon hitting a live wire. She felt as if she and Barry were both tumbling through the air, unable to catch themselves until they landed flat.

Splat.

Whack.

She reached to her temple, massaging one side while cradling the phone against the other. "This has to be stopped." She used her sternest voice.

"Are you going to chain yourself to one of those pecan trees or what?"

"Don't tempt me." Because Danica was so incensed at the moment, she just might do that.

"The contractor is making the decision today." Barry obviously knew a little more than she did, but his passion for the land wasn't nearly as strong.

His only interest was the bottom line. But now wasn't the time to have that debate.

"So," his tone was devoid of the immediacy communicated by his words, "you better be here before he leaves at five o'clock."

"I have to work," she hissed again, willing him to understand.

"This is work."

"But I'm not punching a time clock for it." Another set of footsteps padded past Danica's desk. She turned her head to see behind her, but whichever co-worker was walking had already come and gone. She rededicated herself to a controlled voice as she aimed to wrap up this exchange that wasn't going anywhere.

"I'll do something." Danica just didn't know what.

"You've got until five today." Barry was hanging her and their agreement out to dry. If he weren't so spineless, she wouldn't have to get involved with something that wasn't supposed to be happening anyway.

She blew a hot breath of air against the line, wishing the gust would punch Barry's face and knock some sense into him.

Danica would have never entered into this agreement if she'd known she would have to be the one handling the decisions of the development that—in the long run—really would matter. She was principled when it came to land, and she would be a fighter for doing what she thought was right for the acreage and for future generations of lot owners. That was her approach to development, which she had quickly learned was different than Barry's. All the more reason this would be their first and last partnership on a project.

No more being talked into another with him for the lure of a quick-buck turnaround.

No more headaches from dealing with problems he was too weak to tackle.

This dealing had shown her a whole other side of Barry, and she'd seen his true colors. She better understood the nuances of why he and Paige divorced. She never did fault her friend for that decision. Still, now she was able to comprehend it on a whole new level.

Danica hung up the phone, resolving to focus on her eight-to-five work. But even as she returned e-mails and pushed paperwork, her thoughts turned toward the task that awaited her at the end of the day. She had already taken a half hour here and an hour there out of her work week, so slipping away yet again was going to be tough. Barry should have understood that, but he lacked the perception or the care to do so.

Men. She smacked her lips in disgust trying to rid her mouth of the bitter taste as she thought about her precarious position. If the actions of Barry Van Soyt represented all men in the world, it was enough to sour her on the whole gender.

~*~

Grady's last patient of the day had come and gone.

And he stayed in the exam room, enjoying the silence and the dim lighting that gave his eyes a welcome break from their hard work of the day.

He took his glasses from his face and laid them on the counter. He brought his fingers to the bridge of his nose and squeezed away his stress. It had been a busy workday, but a fulfilling one. Still, he needed a reprieve.

Deep, meditative breaths filled his lungs and lowered his pulse. Just as he was feeling the effects, the door swung open. Iris started into the room and then stopped again. "Sorry. I didn't realize anyone was in here."

"Just having some downtime."

"You deserve it." Iris offered a sympathetic smile. "It's been a long day."

Grady gestured to the wall switch. "You can turn the lights back on."

"Keeping them off is fine." Lower base lighting installed in the room kept a slight glow, avoiding total darkness. "Besides, I actually think I might join you for a moment."

"Everything OK?" Grady picked up his glasses and set them against his eyes again.

"Not really." Iris leaned on the side wall, settling her head against it as if her neck were too tired to hold itself up.

Oh boy. "What's going on?"

Grady was the boss, but he wasn't used to playing armchair psychiatrist when it came to personnel matters. But he needed to get comfortable in such a role, as doing so with certain individuals in this area was a necessity.

"It's Samantha."

Grady straightened his posture. "Is everything OK?"

Iris sighed. "She broke up with her boyfriend."

Grady was even less equipped to handle personal problems than professional ones. "And is that affecting her work?"

Iris shrugged. "You know how she is."

No, he really didn't. As far as Grady was concerned, she was an effective receptionist. She performed the duties of her job, covered others when asked, and handled lots of patient questions and concerns that never made it back to Grady because she resolved them. True, the four of them in Spectacle Optique knew the basics of each other's lives, learning more with each passing month. There may come a day later when he, Heath, Iris, and Samantha were tighter, but Grady certainly wasn't going to push. He had no reason to do that. Work relationships needed to be organic and comfortable, not forced. And he wanted to keep an atmosphere of respect by differentiating their work lives and home lives. But Iris's words were blurring that.

"Is there something I need to know?" He shifted uncomfortably, not sure he should be having this conversation with Iris. It seemed like a privacy invasion of Samantha's, and he debated saying so.

Iris avoided an answer to his question by asking one of her own, musing the words as if they weren't intrusive.

But they were.

"Are you seeing anyone?"

The question stopped a conversation that had barely started.

"Iris," Grady spoke gently, "I'm really not going to answer—"

"I'm not prying. I just want to know if you're seeing someone or not because that affects whether you might understand what Samantha is going through."

"I've certainly had relationships end, if that's what you're wondering."

"Recently?"

This was prying.

Grady stayed silent.

"Because if you're single…"

Grady braced himself for a setup he didn't want to happen. Even thinking about Samantha in that way wasn't on his radar. Again, nice woman, hard worker. Not a love interest.

But this wasn't about Samantha.

Iris pinched a strand of her blonde hair and twirled it. "It might be a good idea for us to do something nice for her. We could find a gesture that would cheer her up. Maybe we can get together tonight away from the office and talk about it?"

Grady…and Iris?

"My apartment's available. That way, we can talk. In private."

This was already more privacy than he should be having with any one employee. An after-hours pairing between them would be stickier than a fudge sundae. "I don't think that's a good idea."

Iris's face fell, and Grady could see the wheels of her mind turning to try another angle.

"But thank you, Iris, for bringing Samantha's situation to my attention." He stood and made a motion toward the door, mustering his most supervisorial demeanor. "I'll make sure I don't bother her with anything unnecessary." And then, to keep Iris busy too, he added, "And I'm sure you'll help me do the same."

Iris's eyes drooped sad as a pound puppy with the realization she wasn't going to be able to take Grady home.

No, he wasn't going home with either of his female co-workers.

Or any female, for that matter.

~*~

Danica made a secret call from a stall of the appraisal district's bathroom to the contractor hired for Cinnamon Ridge, begging him to give her ten minutes of his time after hours to talk trees.

He agreed.

She needed to jet the moment the time clock struck 5:00 p.m. so she could swoop across town and convince him that, while tree removal was going to make heavy equipment easy to come in and out, too many negative consequences hung in the wings. She was prepared to remind him of the way the lots were going to be marketed with the word mature highlighting the trees. While being the contractor offered him some leverage, and their agreement hadn't specified the trees, she was ready to fight this point now.

She finished her work in her cubicle, counted the minutes until quitting time, and then left on the dot. She raced in her car to meet the contractor as she rehearsed her best plea to save the trees.

Danica made the trip in record time and pulled perpendicular to the location, cutting the engine of her car to park it along the asphalt street that would lead into the entrance that was still under development. She and Barry had decided on something conventional yet grand, a stately sign flanked by landscaping and two cinnamon-colored pillar entrances to the subdivision that would match its name. It was taking shape beautifully; the grove of trees near the front and the smattering of other shade offerings made each lot distinct.

She stowed her sunglasses in place, wishing she

had her glasses at this point so the man walking toward her looked less like a blurry Sasquatch and more like a human. She met him halfway in an open space with grass beneath their feet but no shade above. Danica hoped the afternoon heat would help make her point.

Though as she launched into her plea, that small move made little difference. The contractor argued as much. "We've got a lot of concrete to pour. We don't need tree roots bulging any of that and creating cracks that owners will come back to you about." True, that was a headache down the road, which Danica didn't need. "Getting them out of here will make it easier to dig lines, too. Water, sewage, high-speed internet."

"I know." Those merits were hard to debate.

"We've talked about all of this."

"No," she corrected. "You talked to Barry about all of this."

He threw a hand into the air, his frustration evident. "He's an owner, too."

"We're fifty-fifty." She extended her hands with open, upturned palms, practically begging at this point. "Look, let me get Barry on the phone. You'll hear we have a consensus."

He wagged his head, mumbling something indecipherable. Probably it wasn't pleasant, but she also had a contract with him on which they couldn't renege. Not at this point when they were knee-deep in the thick of it all.

Danica didn't wait for him to agree. She punched the call-back number for Barry, initialized speaker phone, and let the contractor hear both of them say the words, "Keep the trees."

"Fine." He wiped his brow. "But if any of them show a single hint of dying, my guys are taking them out."

"Fair." Danica ended the call with Barry, tossed the phone into her purse, and crossed her hands over her chest in satisfaction at what she considered a compromise.

The stifling heat made her as uncomfortable as the encounter. As she pivoted away from the source of her stress and walked back toward her car, she considered how some people were cut out for supervisory roles—and some weren't. There was a time she thought she might be, but this one project had made her realize this was not a strength of hers. This role gave her less gratification than she anticipated.

She hoped it, at least, netted a decent financial return. She would still split the profits with Barry, and initial calculations for a favorable return-on-investment had been positive. Those joys, however, seemed less exciting now than they once had been.

The end of this project couldn't come fast enough for Danica's taste. She was done with this wild hair of a plan, done with trying to broker decisions where she had to twist her only partner's arm for support in the process. Barry Van Soyt could make other plans, but they wouldn't be in partnership with her.

TEN

Glasses should finally help Danica see straight.

She marched back into Spectacle Optique for the fourth time in two weeks, ready to pick up the turquoise frames that she hoped would stop her squinting, minimize her eye strain, and reduce her stress.

"That's a tall order." Heath laughed when she told him the list. "But I think I can deliver on two out of the three of those." He handed the case to her with the glasses inside. "Try 'em on."

Danica brushed her hand across the smooth exterior of the high-end case. She was sure she was somehow paying for it in the cost of the glasses anyway. But Dr. Urban had finagled that generous fifty percent discount. Or had he demanded it when Heath was writing the ticket? And why for her? Danica had wondered that over the week, turning the conversation over in her head as best she could remember, which wasn't saying much. Because all she could recall with absolutely clarity was the way Dr. Urban had sneaked up behind her when she was sitting at the vanity table, eased in her mirrored view, and melted her with brief attention.

She glanced at her reflection today, half expecting

him to make another surprise appearance behind her shoulder. When he didn't, she opened the glasses case and placed them across her eyes, ready for the wonder lenses to do their job.

"How do they feel?" Heath gave her the space to consider them.

Danica turned her head right to left and back again. She looked down and up, judging the fit, "Quite comfortable, actually." The bright color was such a bonus. "I really like the way they look."

"They are a good choice." Heath folded a polishing cloth atop the table and next to a small pump bottle of cleanser. "These are yours, too. You can use them whenever you need to give those lenses a shine."

Heath had her focus on a few different objects to make sure she was comfortable with the change as well as using slightly different angles and her periphery. "You may notice the rim of the glasses now, but you'll get used to it all after just a couple of days."

Danica nodded. There was a learning curve to everything. "If this place had more pictures," she said, noting the blank walls near the patient entrance and by reception, "I would be able to test these better."

"Dr. Urban mentioned he wanted to decorate the place more fully." Aside from the displays and waiting room furniture, there wasn't much else in the redesigned space. Nothing in the way of wall art.

"He should try one of the fine arts festivals in San Antonio." Danica and Paige attended such an event at the city's downtown River Walk last year, and both had purchased an original oil painting for their respective places. "Really responsible prices and a great way to get unique, one-of-a-kind art."

"I'll let him know." Heath continued the small talk while Danica studied the glasses, getting used to their weight and placement. "Is art something that interests you?" he asked.

"Doesn't it interest everybody?" Danica always felt that way about art. She had no particular training or experience, but she appreciated anything that took creative energy. Not all artists, after all, have the guts to let others see something so personal. To her, art was a celebration of the imagination, and anyone who could fill a blank space with inspiration was to be commended.

Heath said he understood the genesis of art as a creative outlet.

Danica concurred. "Creativity should never be overrated." She supported the artistic process by viewing, complimenting, and occasionally purchasing something she could afford, always happy to do so. And San Antonio was a wonderful venue for all three of those.

"I guess I've never taken the time to consider it."

"You should." Danica thought everyone should make time for art in one form or another. "And so should Dr. Urban, if he's thinking of adding something to these walls."

"When is that festival in San Antonio?" Heath inquired.

"They have several." Danica stowed the cleanser and cloth in her purse. "But the one I really enjoy is the

Labor Day Arts and Crafts show."

"I'll tell Dr. Urban about that."

Danica picked up her glasses case. "It's a quick drive and a great event." She thanked Heath for his help with the glasses, checked her reflection one final time, and wore her glasses out of Spectacle Optique.

When she stepped outside, she saw colors in her environment as if everything was waking up all around her. Shapes were sharper, hues were more saturated, edges and outlines were crisper. Like a movie rejuvenated by Technicolor, her eyes were channeling the world in a way she had never seen.

She loved this new view.

~*~

Friday's DEAR time gave Danica a second chance to make a first impression with Owen. She wore her glasses into Mrs. Livingston's classroom where Dr. Urban and a couple of the other mentors were already seated and waiting for their charges.

"Good morning," he signaled.

"Morning." She returned a wave to him and to other volunteers scattered around the room.

As she pulled out the chair from her table to have a seat in the same spot as the previous week, Dr. Urban leaned over from his. "Nice glasses."

She smiled broadly beneath the chic frames and played coy. "I got them from a new place in town."

"Must be an incredible location," he teased back.

She cupped her hand over her mouth, creating a

finger megaphone and joked, "If you're lucky, the doc there may give a steep discount on a whim."

He winked at that comment, a cute gesture that made Danica's stomach do a backflip. She stowed her purse beneath her chair to have a seat.

"You as a walking advertisement was money well spent." Grady stage-whispered back to her.

Their playful dramatics continued. "Is that all I am?" She suspected, however, a pang of truth as an undertone to such a comment. Surely, Dr. Urban couldn't discount every client's glasses into the foreseeable future if he hoped to turn a profit. Or maybe he made more on the clinical end. Danica really had no idea. If he was able to step away, though, for volunteerism, she surmised business must be OK.

Not that the inner workings of Spectacle Optique were any of her concern.

And not that Grady Urban's day-to-day dealings should be either.

Still, she thought about him.

Here.

And there.

Focus, Danica, she chastised herself. The little boy who was arriving soon for reading assistance deserved her complete attention. She didn't need to be distracted by the alluring man next to her.

Yet she was.

Pushing down the rising tide of affection, she swung her legs to face the front of the room and pulled herself into a tighter seated position. With the table top just inches from her ribcage, she now had little room to pivot and look at Grady. At least, that's what she told herself.

With her feelings compartmentalized, she was ready for volunteerism.

"Good morning, everyone." Mrs. Livingston's voice rang through the doorway as she led a row of students in single file behind her. "Students, find your readers." She stepped aside to let them into the room, a current of third graders following protocol that mirrored what they had done exactly one week ago. Their lives at school must be predictable and routine. The electricity in the room increased the moment these buzzy, youthful students made their way around tables and chairs to their respective places.

And then there was Owen.

He shuffled toward Danica with his shoulders hunched forward, uninterested and uneager. She tried to look as approachable as she could with a welcoming smile and eye contact, but his head stayed down. "Good morning, Owen." Her voice rang as she pulled out the chair next to her.

He didn't say a word as he slid into place. He wore the same loose basketball shorts as last week. "Do you have your glasses today?" Danica reached to the corner of her own as a way to announce hers in case he didn't remember. "I brought mine."

He seemed unimpressed. But he did dig his hands into a pocket and fished out his red frames.

So he was listening.

Maybe he was a kid who just needed to warm up. He was slow to converse, but Danica hoped he would be quicker when it came to their activity for the day.

Mrs. Livingston clapped her hands to center the room's attention on her as she explained the directions. Each duo would read one book—twice. The first time, the goal was to flip through the pages, alternating guesses of what would happen in the story only by looking at the pictures. Then, the student would take the lead in reading the story, and mentors were supposed to help with any tough pronunciations. "Also," Mrs. Livingston held up a single slim page of a notepad, "each of you has one sheet on your desk. Write your favorite sentence from the story after you finish. Mentors, you do the same."

Mrs. Livingston's approach, as far as Danica could see, was to focus on strengths when it came to the children's literacy. These tasks of hypothesizing and copying words were ones they could do with confidence, and it didn't highlight their weakness in a way that another approach—like writing down unfamiliar words or stopping the story to check a dictionary—might do. Danica suspected there would be a range of different techniques throughout the year, but so far, she really admired Mrs. Livingston's can-do approach with even the most reluctant readers in the classroom.

And to say Owen was reluctant was an understatement.

Their assigned story was one about a monkey who left his rainforest home to visit a city for the first time— or so that's what the pictures suggested. The monkey had all kinds of quirky adventures before deciding that he missed his family and returned home. Bright scenes and gentle humor made this a fun story, and Danica already spied several sentences in contention for her favorite.

"Want to give this a shot now?" Danica prompted after they had completed their cursory discussion.

Owen closed the book, his actions communicating what his mouth failed to speak.

Danica took a deep breath. She was trying, but she didn't know how to encourage someone who behaved in such a lackluster way. She looked up to find Mrs. Livingston, who was absorbed in helping another duo.

She looked to Grady, who was quietly listening as his petite charge read angelically from the pages.

All around, partners were doing the same. Directions were being followed and progress was being made, except for her table.

Danica exhaled her frustration, refusing defeat. It was one book. She needed to help Owen have success with this, even if it meant going off script from what Mrs. Livingston had planned.

Last week's picture drawing worked, and she thought this week their glasses would be an icebreaker, though Owen hardly noticed her new turquoise frames. Or, if he did, he didn't care. She needed to salvage this session, and she needed to understand Owen.

In a moment that broke her otherwise jovial tone, she asked a straight, no-nonsense question. "Do you like reading?"

Owen returned a no-nonsense answer. "No."

She nodded at his honesty, pleased, at least, that they were having an exchange. But rather than interject her experience or supplant answers of her own, she let him do that. "Can you tell me why?"

Owen pointed to his forehead, the fresh and painful looking scar like a crack across otherwise perfect skin. "Kids have been calling me Humpty Dumpty and saying I can't use my brain anymore."

Danica's heart broke in two, the thoughtless and hurtful words of other children tugging at her. How cruel some kids could be. No matter how innocuous they thought their words were, what they communicated could certainly leave a big impact. She saw that fact written all across Owen's crestfallen face.

Danica pushed the book aside, wanting to show Owen that he had her complete attention. "That's awful of them to say." She let empathy guide her. "When did you hurt your head?"

He averted his gaze from Danica. "This summer. Riding my bike." He kept his voice low.

"That must have been very scary." She validated Owen's feelings in that moment, even without knowing the full story.

Owen shrugged. "I don't remember the hospital."

So the injury was serious enough to require a visit. The wound sure looked like it, though Danica was no expert. "Not remembering some things is OK."

He nodded.

"You were a brave kid." Danica's mind flashed to Paige's experience when Nathan was two years old and was hospitalized for appendicitis. Though there's truth in the adage that kids are resilient, their strength in times of crisis should not be overlooked. She wanted Owen to know that. "There's no good reason for calling people names, especially when they act like superheroes instead of eggheads."

Those words actually made Owen laugh, and that tiny bit of meaningful interaction fueled Danica further as she insisted Owen was not an egghead. "Don't believe any kid who calls you one. Or any other name, for that matter."

She wanted to wrap him in her arms in a tight and supportive hug to let him know that he mattered. But as much as her heart tugged in that direction, her head reminded her of the public-school setting. The last thing she wanted to do was violate a rule or make Owen uncomfortable. She continued with words instead, using them to build him up. "You have a brain inside of that head that was protected in your bike accident, and that's such an important thing. You," she underscored, "are important. And we're going to work together to exercise that brain by reading so that you can get stronger and stronger there."

"But that's the problem," he revealed. "Sometimes my brain hurts."

An orchestra of thoughts ran through Danica's own head. Some rang with concern, others chimed with questions. Was the school aware of his summer accident? Had the doctor diagnosed Owen with a concussion? Or was there some other trauma that was causing his head pain? She could ask Mrs. Livingston, but now wasn't the time.

Still, she wanted to make sure Owen was all right in this moment. "Does your brain hurt now?"

"No, not now."

That relieved a bit of Danica's worry. "OK then. How about we stretch that brain little by little, page by page? You can start, and I'll be here sending shared brain power your way as you read so we can finish this book together."

Talk of good vibrations seemed to be the ticket. Owen nodded, flipped the book around, and began from page one. To Danica's surprise, he read through the entire book without stopping.

Danica wondered if Owen had weaknesses with literacy, or if the reason for his placement in DEAR was accident-related. After the end of their allotted time and once all the kids had exited the room, she stayed to ask Mrs. Livingston. Danica had her new glasses, but she still needed to see straight as far as Owen was concerned.

ELEVEN

Grady pushed his chair back at the end of the forty-minute DEAR time and helped Alexis do the same. "Thanks for your hard work today."

She stood first and flashed another toothless grin.

"Before I forget, I have something for you." Grady reached into the pocket of his Oxford shirt and procured a pad of paper.

"What's that?" Alexis's eyes shone with curiosity as he clicked a ball-point pen.

Grady scribbled a few words on the top sheet. "Do you remember me telling you I'm a doctor?"

Alexis nodded.

"Doctors write prescriptions to help people." This was easy logic for an elementary student. Grady tore the sheet from the pad and handed it to Alexis. "And this is going to be your prescription."

Alexis tilted her head and read the words, instructing her to read for twenty minutes every day. Writing a book prescription for Alexis was something he thought might help her remember to practice a little bit every day. "You can read anything you can get your hands on. Library books, comics, the back of a cereal box. Deal?"

Her returned smile sealed the doctor's orders.

She hugged the piece of paper when Mrs. Livingston announced that all the kids should line up. "Prepare for your homerooms. Make sure you didn't leave anything behind." At that prompting, Alexis made a final move. She turned to Grady and opened her arms for an instant, unexpected bear hug around his waist. The surprise rocked Grady's balance, and he was unsure how to respond.

"See you next week." More than her hug, those words were as big of a surprise because Samantha had volunteered to take the slot the following week. He hadn't explained that to Alexis, nor had he even had time to share the plan with Mrs. Livingston.

Instead, Grady managed to squeak a simple "OK" before Alexis's show of affection ended as swiftly as it began. She released her grip around his waist and spun to follow Mrs. Livingston's edict.

"Impressive." Danica observed from a few feet away.

Grady stayed still as a statue, reeling from the shock of the eight-year-old's actions. "Not something I expected."

"That pretty much characterizes my whole meeting with Owen today." She spoke with resignation.

"Troubled by something?"

"I need to talk with Mrs. Livingston about Owen." Danica grabbed her purse.

A quick chat with Mrs. Livingston was in order for him as well, but how could he now disappoint Alexis when she expected to see him next week? Grady would sort that later. Right now, it seemed as though Danica had a bigger challenge. Her slow start with Owen today was something Grady noted in between glances while he worked with Alexis. Owen was more standoffish than the other children. "Is he still not warming up?"

"There's more to it than that." Danica furrowed her brow as if in thought about the entire situation. From Grady's vantage point, Owen and Alexis were polar opposites when it came to personality. But they were in the same grade and this same reading program, so maybe there was some commonality. Talking through that may help, and he told Danica so. "I'm no expert, but I'm happy to listen."

"That's very kind of you." Still, her attention slid to Mrs. Livingston, who was walking to the front of the students' single file line to open the classroom door.

"But getting a teacher's guidance is best. She's the expert." Grady filled in the words he suspected Danica failed to say.

Danica's face lit in lightbulb thought. "But so is a doctor."

Grady didn't follow. "What was that?"

"A doctor! An expert! Why didn't I think of that before? Owen needs someone to address his head trauma."

He saw wheels of recognition turning in her eyes, her mind powering her into an idea. "He needs someone at the school to get that ball rolling."

Communication between doctors and teachers was always wise, and part of his thinking behind the book prescription he slid to Alexis was a way to bridge that divide in the home environment. So if a child had an accident that affected his brain, like perhaps Owen did, it was especially important for the school to address that.

Danica certainly thought so. "Remember when I hit my head?"

"How could I forget?" Iris had planted more worry about legal recourse with Grady when the paperwork came through for Danica's glasses. She made an off-handed remark about keeping extra copies in case of any lawsuit. Grady wanted to dismiss the event, but Iris insisted he not forget it. Now, here was Danica plopping it into plain conversation.

"I was already anxious when that happened, and that bump set me back."

Maybe Iris was right. Grady memorized the words Danica spoke. Listening wasn't enough. He needed to remember in case there was a need to resurface this conversation for legal purposes down the road. He had a real interest in Danica, but he needed to stay mindful of business interests as well.

"So I hit my head, and I couldn't think straight."

Grady didn't dare interrupt for fear of turning the tide of this one way or another. He instead offered verbal listener noise but nothing further.

"Cloudy head space is no way to exist."

He could relate. Grady's own head fogged with concern of how far Danica would push.

"So if a head is injured, that's going to affect the mind. At least for the short term, right?"

Grady hesitated to commit with anything beyond "mm, hmm."

The last of the children exited the room. Danica turned to him with a sharp pivot of direction, both in body and words. "Owen had an accident." She pointed to her own forehead. "You saw his scar?"

"That injury is hard to miss." He'd seen it the first time Owen entered the room. It led the way as he walked, the red and slightly raised skin an immediate medical indicator of the scar's newness.

"Right." Danica hugged her purse close. "And I think there's something to consider between that injury, his glasses, and his reading skills."

"Do you mean delay in comprehension? Something residual from his accident?"

Danica said that could be a possibility. "Or maybe just mental fatigue."

"That might be widespread with elementary kids as a whole," he warned, thinking about the other lackadaisical looks he saw some of the kids wear.

Danica shook her head. "I don't buy that."

Fair enough. She didn't have to.

"I don't know Owen well at all." With only two visits, not enough time had passed for any adults in the room to make such a claim with the kids. "But I know that after I blacked out, my mind was a little jumbled."

Grady hoped that wasn't the case for long. He had no metric for response if it did, yet he braced for hearing the worse as she continued. Perhaps Iris was right that it was best to stay alert to something residual from Danica's fall.

Instead, Danica swerved away from personal reflection and back to her student. "Owen's accident was so much worse than a little fall. So even now, his brain might just be exhibiting symptoms from his accident."

With Danica's own accident fresh on his mind, he asked about Owen's. "How long ago was it?"

"Sometime over the summer. He didn't tell me exactly."

Grady suspected there wasn't time enough in their weekly forty minutes for much detail.

"But concussions come in varying degrees," Danica continued, explaining that she had read some information about them online. "And effects can range all over the place. It's hard to be certain of what causes what."

Uncertainty was Iris's caution to Grady. She'd warned him of Danica being affected by more than she let on that day in the office. Iris was convinced that a new patient like Danica was someone who might milk an injury, especially when time passed long enough to let an idea manifest. Grady had blown off her words, yet now, as he stood by Danica, he found himself reminded of Iris's warning just the same.

She pinched her necklace pendant between two fingers and slid it against the length of the silver chain. She spoke in between the movement. "I know DEAR time is valuable for any kid, but I want to make sure he's not misdiagnosed here. I need to ask Mrs. Livingston about this."

Grady's analysis shifted from past to present. Two

weeks ago, Danica was a stranger who entered his office colored by anxiety and a bit of clumsiness. But here, she was clear-headed and determined. Grady admired her focus in closing any gap of learning for Owen. Fact-finding through the teacher was an admirable first step. It was selfless to boot.

And only selfish people sued for hitting their head in a medical office, right?

Mrs. Livingston was out of sight at the moment, but she'd be available again once all the kids were delivered to their classrooms. All the other adult volunteers exited in time, some waving good-bye to Danica and Grady and others slipping out in the same silence in which they came. They would sign-out at the office and be on their way.

Grady needed to be too, but he didn't want to leave Danica on an uncertain note. Nor did he want her to be alone in a room. There was a level of concern he was trying to sort, though how much of it was personal and how much was directed at Danica, he wasn't sure. Earlier when Alexis hugged him, he had been concerned about how to react. But that was a very small act. Danica wasn't dealing with a hug. Owen's medical history added a whole different reason to be concerned. Yet Grady suspected, just like there were privacy protocols in a medical office, there were similar ones in a public classroom. "Can a teacher share a student's personal information with you?"

"I'll find out." Danica dropped her hands from her necklace and swung her purse to her side. "The least I can do is ask."

At that, Grady saw virtue in Danica, an attractive characteristic. He had already seen her often enough outside the office that he was now beginning to see her as more than a client. She showed different layers, her personality and attributes unmasking in a way that Grady enjoyed witnessing. Volunteerism and mentorship were admirable enough, but now she aimed to track down answers that showed desire beyond helping at a surface level. She cared to make a difference, and helping in a meaningful way mattered to Danica Lara.

Grady basked in the wake of her selflessness, watching her approach Mrs. Livingston with a projectile focus in an effort to understand—and help—Owen. He continued to admire her willingness to get involved and make a difference as he waited in the wings of the classroom, far enough away to give them privacy but close enough in case Danica needed him afterward.

What he saw in Danica that day was what he looked for in hiring medical professionals. Strong moral fortitude was what he sought in the very best of candidates within the medical field, but seeing it manifest outside of that delighted him as much as Danica herself was beginning to do.

~*~

Danica had a hard time focusing on her work back at the appraisal district.

Mrs. Livingston had been helpful enough,

responding to her queries about Owen's summer bicycle accident with, "The school nurse is aware of his injury" and "the counselor has paperwork on file from his surgeon." Ultimately, however, Mrs. Livingston contended that "Owen's need for one-on-one help is not accident-related. He had poor reading scores last year, and he needs shoring-up so he doesn't fail the state standardized test required of all students at the end of the year."

"Is that the goal?" Danica didn't realize the DEAR program had such a prescriptive end-game.

"He needs to pass," Mrs. Livingston argued.

Passing a test, though, and learning the fundamentals of reading—and the joy of it—were very different goals as far as Danica was concerned. She liked reading articles online and getting lost in an occasional novel on weekends, especially to pass the time of being alone. Book boyfriends and far-flung tales took her mind off relationships she didn't have.

Mrs. Livingston, in her infinite elementary wisdom, must have suspected what Danica was thinking. "If it makes you feel better, I hardly think about those tests. They become buzz words and talking points within the school. I just want DEAR time to be fun for students. I know it makes a difference for them."

Danica nodded, not wanting to get caught up in policy or semantics. She knew she could mentor, and that would ultimately impact Owen in some way. Even if she wasn't able to bridge an understanding of his accident, she could build his literacy and confidence week to week. She was committed to that.

"I'm so pleased to hear that." Mrs. Livingston beamed when she told her. She thanked her on the way out, and Grady had walked with her to the office, signed-out, and escorted her through the front door to her car in one of the visitor's spots near where he also parked. They talked about going back to work and the quick pace of their Friday workday in light of the mentorship that made the morning fly.

Away from the bustle of the elementary school and the buzz of a man near here, her mind nonetheless kept finding its way in flashbacks to the morning. She removed her hands from her computer's keyboard and rocked back in her rolling desk chair with only her thoughts.

"Danica," a voice broke her daydreaming. She swiveled to see Cameron, her boss with an androgynous name and a gravelly voice to match. Plenty of taxpayers called the office, unsure of whether Cameron was to be addressed as a male or female. With Danica and the rest of her coworkers, she was on a first-name basis. But the tough-as-nails supervisor had everyone toeing the line of polite interaction.

"Yes, Cameron?" She spun, sitting up straight against the back of her swivel chair at the command of her voice.

"Someone came into the office looking for you this morning." She wasted no time in addressing the situation that prompted the visit to Danica's cubicle.

"Oh?" Danica reminded Cameron about the elementary school commitment, though she was pretty sure Cameron had seen her leave on the way out anyway.

But this wasn't about that situation. "We need to have a talk about personal situations interfering with work."

Danica started to open her mouth in protest about the elementary school not being personal. It was as much a community service project as, say, the office's holiday food drive or the time employees spent selling benefit dinners or raffle tickets from their service windows.

"Barry Van Soyt came by looking for you." Cameron gave no opportunity for explanation.

Just my misfortune. The one person in her life who sometimes acted elementary was muddying her work waters yet again. Danica snapped her mouth shut like a steel trap to keep from reacting.

"You can do what you want on your own time. I know all about Cinnamon Ridge."

Of course, she would know about that. It wasn't as if Danica could keep land development a secret in her line of work. Those beans spilled the moment she signed the deed paperwork with Barry as buyer for the property they were subdividing.

She hadn't talked about it with Cameron or anyone else at the office since it was, after all, a personal project. Even so, Cameron knew, evidenced by this tart, one-sided conversation that was making Danica shift in her seat.

"Do not conduct personal business on work time. Certainly not when you're collecting a county paycheck. Understood?"

"Yes, ma'am." Danica wanted to shrink unto herself with embarrassment at being called out.

But being called out would have been much better than Cameron's next move.

"I have this written warning for you." She produced a paper from a manila envelope scissored between her fingers. "You will need to read it, sign it, and I'll file it for personnel purposes."

A warning? Documented? In four years, Danica had never been delivered such a blow. Granted, Cameron had only been the chief appraiser for half the time of Danica's employment, but even before the previous appraiser's retirement, she never had a supervisor warning, never even a poor annual review.

She reached with tepid fingers to grasp the paper that she wanted to ball up and throw away in disgust.

"You'll note today's date."

That was the absolute last concern Danica had.

"I haven't recorded the other times I've seen Barry in here on loose business that I'm sure didn't really involve a need for county services. I've also got a list of the times he's telephoned you on your cell during work hours."

How could she have that information? But Danica had no room to argue, for the accusations were true. She shrank in further humiliation. Obviously, she wasn't as discreet as she thought she was.

The potential for profit had blinded her to professional obligations, and she signed the work reprimand in defeat. She handed the paper back to

Cameron.

"Need I remind you of this line again?" Cameron asked.

"No ma'am." Point made, notice taken.

"Good." Cameron slid the paper back into the manila envelope and left Danica alone.

Shame was her only company for the rest of the day.

TWELVE

White was Grady's favorite color.

And it wasn't for reasons other people might think.

Each wall in Spectacle Optique's retail space, waiting area, and patient hallway were painted a creamy, soothing ivory. Grady Urban's vision could sometimes be on overdrive, and walking past blank walls created a break for his eyes. He loved his career, but like anyone, he needed some escape now and again.

However, explaining that to others in general wasn't a task he cared to undertake. The few people outside his field with whom he had tried to talk about the strains of optometry didn't really get it. Some people even poked fun at him without realizing their comments were hurtful, like asking if he was able to see in X-ray vision. He wasn't some trick pony. And, sometimes, ill-thought gifts or outreaches just made it all worse—like one former girlfriend who thought it was funny to give him a set of children's coloring books as a gift.

They weren't very serious as a couple, at least not at the point when the gift was given for his birthday. But she'd made some tacky comments about how hard it was to shop for a doctor and about the boredom optometrists must face, that revealed she really didn't understand much about his job. She also didn't seem to care to, so their relationship took a nosedive and never really recovered.

It ended.

Since being in Seguin and starting his business, Grady had been so busy that contentment was in his work. Unlike with a girlfriend, he didn't have to explain anything in grave detail to his employees. They didn't press him. They didn't have to know he gazed at patients' eyes longer than most optometrists so that his own vision could focus; they could think he was just a thorough medical professional. They didn't have to know that he sometimes closed his eyes to give his receptors a break; they could continue to think he took a meditative breather once in a while. They didn't have to know that he secretly liked white walls; they could think he just didn't have much interest in art.

But Heath had a plan about that.

"I think you should dress these walls," he told Grady at the end of one workday, gesturing to the blank spaces they passed in the hallway.

"Really?" Grady stopped as Heath did, and they faced one another.

"Yeah," he said, as if choosing and hanging art was no big deal.

Maybe to most people it wasn't.

"We've been in this space long enough now," Heath continued. "The waiting room is fine because of the displays, but something along here,"—he made a sweeping motion down the hall—"might make this more welcoming when people turn the corner."

It was like a blank canvas—and Grady liked it for that reason. "You don't think that would be distracting?"

"I think you need something distracting." He brought his hand to rest on the column that jutted awkwardly into the space, the same one Danica had run into weeks ago, and that had been a close call for numerous other patients. "At the very least, hang something here."

"Like what?" A big stop sign? Caution tape?

"A canvas. Nothing bulky." He turned as if imagining something.

Grady followed Heath's gaze.

"What's going on?" Iris triangulated behind them.

"I'm trying to convince Dr. Urban we could use some color against these walls."

"Oooh!" Iris cooed and brought her hands together in a happy clap. "Design time!"

Heath held his palm against the brick horizontally and then vertically, marking a general size and insisting "no bigger than this" and "something universal."

"Absolutely. I vote for something fun, maybe something abstract. Very modern, very chic."

Abstract paintings were Grady's least favorite, and that was no judgment against their artistic quality. The layering of colors and the bright splashes always made his eyes overload. Sometimes, the size of the canvas itself was enough to make Grady dizzy if he stared too long. He much preferred soothing watercolors of simple objects or easy landscapes. Those, though, he knew were not always in universal taste.

In Iris's excitement, she took a complete turn with another idea. "Or movie posters! Framed, glossy marques all up and down this space." She lit up as if she were walking the red carpet. "We could rotate the selection."

Heath was a known movie buff, so he liked the idea. "That would be pretty cool."

"Or vintage!" Iris absorbed herself into DIY mode with a flood of continued ideas.

After several minutes of battling their merits, Heath finally turned to Grady for a verdict. "So what do you think?"

I think I need to make my employees happy and my customers happy. But not at the expense of my own eyes. "I need to see some art." He didn't want to commit to any decision, especially on the spot.

"You're in luck!" Heath said he knew of an upcoming art show in San Antonio.

"Sounds expensive," Grady hedged. He already had so much money invested in the building.

"Not what you think. This is affordable art, local artists showing what they've done. Not inflated, stuffy metropolitan gallery price tags."

That interested Grady as an option. "When's the show?"

"I think Danica said it was over the Labor Day weekend."

"Danica?" Iris questioned Heath before Grady had

a chance to do so.

"Yes, you remember." He edged Iris with a verbal reminder. "Danica Lara. She was in here a couple of weeks ago."

Grady glanced at Iris, and he knew the look she was making. He had seen it worn on a few women during relationships. There was no mistaking Iris's soured look of jealousy at the mention of an attractive female's name.

"You could probably call her up and ask her for more information," Heath continued, oblivious to what Grady saw.

"Or look online," Iris countered quickly. "There's no reason to bother someone when the Internet shows that information. I can even look with you."

Grady knew what Iris was doing. He wasn't, though, going to make any move in Iris's direction, nor would he let her try to do the same. Office romances were completely out of the question.

But an opposite sex friendship with a patient was a different story.

They didn't know Grady was seeing Danica on a weekly basis at Seguin Elementary School. He planned to talk with Samantha anyway about taking her slot for this upcoming Friday because he was already committed to Alexis, not wanting to disappoint the little girl who expected him to be there. But he also liked being able to see Danica. There was something growing between them, not yet in the arena of romance, but Grady wasn't sure if he wanted that added to the equation. Sure, his focus was on his business, yet he and Danica always seemed to have an easy exchange. That was new and unexpected territory for him.

Aside from general conversation, they had the commonality of their volunteerism through SES. Still, he didn't want to overthink it, nor did he want to undertake art selection at the moment.

"Thanks, both of you, for giving me some ideas." He was glad his employees continued to casually share their thoughts. He wanted to provide that environment for them, a two-way street of communication. "I'll think about it."

He also wanted to ask Danica. That could wait until Friday.

Couldn't it?

As Grady readied to leave for the day and was alone in the office before evening lockup, a yearning to contact Danica trumped the possibility of waiting.

He reached for his phone.

~*~

Danica unlocked her car, swung her purse over the console, and sank into the driver's seat as her weekend began.

Finally.

She kicked off her heels and the stress of the day and hooked her index finger through the ankle straps before tossing them into the backseat. She started the ignition, revved the air conditioner to full blast, and ratcheted the volume of her car stereo to let the sounds of the latest pop song wash over her. Perhaps cool air and a catchy chorus could help her forget Cameron's reprimand.

Not quite. Even as she closed her eyes to rest her head, her boss's words still rang, an uncomfortable rattling of her professional confidence. She had been tempted not to sign the warning that would become part of her permanent record. But refusal would have made the situation worse.

Later that afternoon, she was still second-guessing her acquiescence. Regret was replaced by a biting temptation to sneak into Cameron's file cabinet and make that reprimand disappear.

Ultimately, though, the hours paced by, and Danica completed her duties as she did every day, shuffling the paperwork that moved like molehills desk-to-desk and answering e-mails with laser focus before happily hitting delete to clear her inbox.

As cool air and tunes streamed through her car's interior, her cell phone's ringtone joined the sounds. Danica opened her eyes, hoping it wasn't Barry with some ridiculous eleventh-hour work week crisis involving Cinnamon Ridge. She fished the phone from her purse, guided by the sound as she wrapped her fingers around the screen and slid her thumb to accept the call. She brought the phone to her ear just before the call would have headed to voicemail. "Hello?"

"Danica?" The voice wasn't Barry's. "Can you hear me OK?"

Danica dialed down the stereo's volume, replacing the pop star songbird's voice with her own. "Hi, yes."

But who was this?

"I hope I'm not calling at a bad time. Are you still at work?"

Danica leveled her gaze to scan the parking lot. "Not exactly." The voice on the other end of the line sounded familiar, but she still couldn't quite place it. "I'm sorry," she apologized for her lack of clarity in the moment. "Who is this?"

A light chuckle tumbled through the speaker and into her ear. "Sorry about that. Five o'clock hits, and I totally lose my manners. It's Dr. Urban. Grady," he added, underscoring the call as personal.

Danica reached to the corner of her glasses, tipping them back in reaction to hearing from the optometrist. "Is everything OK?"

"Yes, oh yes, of course."

She now recognized Dr. Urban's voice, but there was a nervousness as he spoke that was uncharacteristic.

"This is my cell phone, not the office phone," he added, and then began to explain that he had a question for her about art.

Danica dipped her head to hold the phone against her shoulder as a tingling rushed through her. "Art?" She adjusted an air vent, trying to cool herself as much from the surprise as from actual heat inside the car.

His words, like a paintbrush against a blank canvas, formed an image for her.

"I've been wanting to add some pieces to the office walls, and Heath said that you had knowledge of an art show happening in San Antonio. You mentioned it to him?"

"I know about it if that's what you mean."

"That's more than I know," he countered.

Danica didn't want Grady mistaking her for an art aficionado and said as much.

"But you've been before?"

"Yes."

That seemed to be enough for Grady. "Can you tell me about it?"

Danica flashed back to the trips she made to shows in the past, mainly with Paige and sometimes with a couple of their other friends. "It's a great place to spend a few hours and appreciate the work of local artists. It doesn't take much to support them, and there's probably something for everyone."

"What kind of paintings do you like best?"

"Whatever strikes me." Danica was an equal-opportunity art lover. "I don't discriminate." Last year, one gallery owner had shown Danica and Paige incredible desk-sized pencil sketches with neon mattings. They each purchased one individually, happy to find something that suited them both. She relayed the story to Grady as she also shared where the sketch went. "It's framed in my cubicle. It adds a bright spot to drab days."

"That's exactly what I want to do. I want to find something I personally like that would also be appropriate for the office."

Danica wasn't sure how she fit into this equation. "And I'd be a good judge of that?"

"You've been to the show, so you know what

kinds of things to expect. And you've been to the optometry office."

She turned the words over in her head. Not exactly a one-in-a-million combination. "I don't want to pick something by myself. I could use the extra set of eyes."

If that was not a classic line from an optometrist, Danica didn't know what was. "You're making quite a case here."

As if sensing her slide toward acceptance, Grady talked details. "It's a four-day event the week after this, and since both our offices are closed on the weekend, what do you think about going on Saturday?"

That's when she and Paige went last year, though they made no plans for this year's event since Paige, Everett, and Nathan were headed to Amarillo to visit family over the three-day Labor Day weekend this year. "Saturday is probably the busiest day."

"Isn't that a good thing? The more people, the better the atmosphere and the deals?"

Did Grady know how shows worked at all? His naïveté was the selling point.

"Yes, I'll go."

"You'll do it?" His voice rose in victory.

"I'm not buying you any art," she teased.

"I'll do the buying," Grady clarified. "You just be the eyes."

Danica smiled at his words, and she clicked off the call with future plans and a present upturn to her day that she never would have expected. It almost made her forget the slap of a written reprimand.

Who was she kidding? Nothing could make her

forget that, not even a loud radio techno song that she cranked on the way out the parking lot as she headed home to escape the work week.

She was tempted to drive by Spectacle Optique, though she wasn't sure why. To see Grady? To check whether he was in the parking lot sitting in his own driver's seat making a string of calls to more than one woman? And why would she care if he did? This was a free country, and he was a man who could call whomever he liked.

"But he chose to call me," she whispered as she drove.

And that alone was the most pleasant surprise of Danica's day.

After an easy ten-minute drive, Danica arrived home. She walked into her weekend carrying her heels by their ankle straps over her shoulder. Padding into the house, she tossed the shoes on the floor and her purse on the couch, swaying her hips as she moved to the beat of a song still lingering in her head. She lit a scented candle and kept the lights of her living room dim, basking in the calm atmosphere. She loved coming home, a complete one-hundred-eighty-degree turn from the stress of her week.

Grady's voice accompanied Danica in her mind, even as she moved through her house. She couldn't shake their conversation or the quiet thrill that built regarding their plans for next week. They hadn't set a time, but as she processed the possibilities, there was certainly the chance that a couple of hours strolling through galleries and street exhibitors would lead to vendor booths of food and drink. Maybe they'd sit together and have a beverage. Perhaps share a meal. Laugh together in conversation.

Hold hands.

Danica rolled her shoulders, shrugging off the late afternoon dreaming that was moving too fast. She poured herself a glass of iced tea in the kitchen to cool her thoughts.

Yet Grady was there in her mind.

She brought the rim of the glass to her lips, draining a good portion of the liquid in one long sip. She had a desire to quench more than just her thirst.

She lowered the beverage, resting one hand against the kitchen counter as she gazed out mini-blinded windows to a well-kept backyard that she failed to use often enough. She had a small concrete patio with a four-chair bistro set that didn't get enough use. Hedgerows framed three sides of the privacy fence, shielding the yard from neighbors and their prying eyes.

Danica glanced at the wall clock as an idea formed.

Taking inventory of the refrigerator, pantry, and her cocktail supplies, she was certain she could throw something together. And her friends weren't picky anyway.

That was one of the reasons those gals stayed her friends. She glanced over the relative cleanliness of the space before doing the same in the living room and bathroom. Her house wouldn't pass a hospital-grade inspection, but it was in great shape for Paige, Katrina, and Esmee. She grabbed her phone, texted the trio, and readied for an impromptu girls' night in.

THIRTEEN

Paige, Katrina, and Esmee were as excited to receive Danica's text as she was to send it. They each replied with their own version of "We're in!" one by one.

Paige and Esmee had young kids at home, but their respective husbands were happy to take the reins for an evening. Esmee, a stay-at-home mom, was especially glad to get out of the house. "An excuse to put on a dress!"

Esmee's newborn was the latest reminder to Danica that some of her friends were in committed relationships and starting families of their own. But all of them kept having to remind Esmee not to lose herself to her child.

"We don't have to be your excuse for a dress." Danica made sure to reply to Esmee's text with a winking emoji. Even so, she was glad for her friend's excitement.

Danica was ready to relax over drinks, snacks, and conversation. Decompressing from the stress of the work week with her girlfriends was time well spent. But as much as relaxation was at the forefront, Danica also wanted to debrief from Grady's call. Esmee may not see through her mommy fog enough to offer much in the way of explanation, but perhaps Paige and Katrina could weigh-in with an analysis in a way that perhaps Danica had overlooked.

Whatever the outcome, they would need sustenance to help them. First, Danica checked her stash of beverages for soda and seltzer. Then, she checked the fridge. There was a fresh lemon she could slice along with a jar of olives she recovered from the back shelf. All the ingredients for mocktail drinks!

She lowered her set of four martini glasses from a high shelf along with the stainless-steel cocktail shaker. Bending to the cabinet below, she slid a slate cheese plate and a bamboo cutting board from their slots. A Texas-shaped serving bowl rounded out the containers she needed.

Danica's foodie fetish for artisan cheeses resulted in her always having a tasty selection on hand. She grabbed a triangle of Gorgonzola, her favorite soft Camembert, aged Cheddar yet to be opened, and a nub of firm Manchego. She angled the cheeses around the board before searching her pantry for something to fill in the gaps and provide extra visual and taste bud appeal.

"Bingo!" She grabbed a jar of roasted almonds, two snack-sized boxes of dried cranberries, and a baking bag of dark chocolate chips. Sprinkling the chocolate first, she arranged the rest of the snacks in small mounds, creating an attractive presentation.

"All this needs is a couple of spreaders." She murmured directions to herself as she procured two from the back of her utensil drawer. She cut a cucumber into rounded circles and added what was left of a half bag of baby carrots on the bamboo tray. She slid a container of hummus next to it, pleased with that impromptu appetizer as well. Crispy tortilla chips poured into the heart of Texas completed the spread.

Danica dusted her hands on a dishtowel, admiring how everything came together on such short notice. She never understood people who made a fuss about visitors and having enough food. It doesn't take much to make most people happy.

It certainly didn't for her today. Cameron's reprimand was almost enough to completely ruin her day. And it would have, had she not gotten the phone call from Grady, giving her new focus—as well as this reason to get together with her friends. She wanted their take on their art show plans. Friendly? Romantic? Should she even try to read into them, or was that overthinking the whole thing?

The questions would have to wait until the girls arrived. With the food set, Danica needed to ready herself just the same. She dashed to her bedroom to perform a quick change into a more relaxing outfit. Snapping a pair of black leggings from a drawer and yanking an off-the-shoulder lounge tee from its hanger in her bedroom closet, she cozied into the outfit before finger combing her hair into a French twist and securing it with a jaw clip. Her dark hair cascaded in effortless loose waves from the top of the clip, keeping the weight off her neck.

In her bedroom mirror, she turned her head right and left to check her reflection. Her turquoise glasses looked super-chic with the easy ensemble.

She was getting used to her glasses. Sure, she was glad for the sharpening of her vision. But one aspect she noticed, which her optometrist didn't have to mention, was their visual appeal. They added interest to an outfit in a way she hadn't expected. She was almost feeling guilty that she was enjoying the accessorizing angle.

Almost. She pushed a half-fallen strand of hair back into place before resetting the frames into their perfect position atop her ears. If only Grady could see her now.

~*~

Bands of laughter spread between the four friends as the sun set against a pink sky silhouetted by the shade trees that stretched toward the horizon from Danica's yard. The women dished on snacks and gossip around the outdoor bistro table.

"Let's toast." Paige raised her glass first. "To getting together and getting—"

"Drunk!" Katrina joked, raising her glass high in an exaggerated stretch that prematurely clinked into Paige's.

"I was going to say relaxed." Paige nipped Katrina on the shoulder with a pinch. Both of them were far from drunk since there was no alcohol in their drinks, and getting close to it wasn't their style anyway. Maybe years ago, but now they all reveled in the pleasurable escape of safe drinks with friends who knew better because they watched alcoholic revelry from their early twenties fade in the rearview mirrors that held their pasts. Present company—and controlled drinking—was much more fun on an otherwise uneventful night like their present Friday.

"You're right." Katrina inched her glass closer to Paige's for a redo. "To relaxation!" Danica and Esmee joined their glasses in the air for clinks in shared expression. They each celebrated with another sip.

Esmee licked a residual drop of liquid from her lips. "You make a good mocktail martini, Danica."

"Here, here!" Katrina raised her glass again in toast as Danica took a seated bow.

Esmee set her glass on the tabletop, circling its rim with the pad of her finger as she admitted, "Any cocktail these days is a good cocktail."

Paige picked up on her tone. "Needing a little down time with a baby in the house?" Paige was the most likely of the bunch to understand the challenges of a child changing the dynamic within a house.

"I love her so much," Esmee began. "But I'm also exhausted."

"It gets easier," Paige counseled, her eyes shining in sympathy as she placed her hand atop Esmee's and gave it a squeeze.

"I don't have a baby and I get exhausted," Katrina challenged the mothers.

"Oh, you just wait." Esmee raised the finger that was toying with the rim of the glass and wagged it instead in warning. "This is a whole other level of exhaustion."

Danica popped an olive into her mouth, chewing before adding her two cents to the conversation. "That's why cosmetic companies make eye creams, right?"

Esmee and Paige both dismissed the words with a grunt. "As if you need an eye cream."

"I didn't say I did." She lowered her glasses on her nose, giving the girls a solid view of her skin. "Taut and flawless, right?"

"I can't see beyond those expensive frames. What are those anyway? Made out of crushed gemstones or something?" Katrina teased.

Danica slid the glasses back into place atop her nose with cool confidence as she said the name of the designer.

"Did the new doctor talk you into spending a fortune on those or what?" Katrina swirled her drink round and round in tight circles above the top of the table, shifting the conversation.

Esmee leaned forward with gossipy interest. "Tell me about the new doctor. Is he hot?"

Danica set her drink between her friends and their prying questions. "Whoa. Let's put the brakes on—"

"So there is something to this doctor?" Esmee's eyes lit with further intrigue.

"There is," Paige answered for Danica.

"Shhh!" Danica shushed her friend, but it was too late.

"Cat's out of the bag!" Katrina sang. "Spill it."

Esmee pouted. "Oh, please spill it. Yes, yes, yes."

"What makes you so interested?" Of all her

friends, Danica didn't expect Esmee to be so absorbed in this banter.

"I spend my days surrounded by diapers." She reached for a handful of chips. "Literal dirt. Give me some figurative dirt."

Katrina set a soft fist against the table as she pounded out a "Dirt! Dirt! Dirt!" challenge.

There wasn't much dirt, and Danica said so. "But he did ask me about the art show in San Antonio next weekend."

"See? Dirt!" Katrina snapped her fingers in victory. "A date!"

"I don't know if it's a date," Danica hemmed. She explained why.

"It's been so long since I've been asked on a date, I don't even think I'd recognize the shape of one," Katrina complained. "I've been single so long I'm surprised nuns haven't come calling to my door."

Paige rolled her eyes. "I don't think that's how it works."

Esmee would have none of these interruptions, shushing the others like they were interrupting a movie she was watching. "Get back to the doctor."

"Dr. McHottie!" Paige chimed in, much to the oohs and aahs of the others while Danica chastised her friend for the more public use of that pet name. "Well, you said he was hot."

"I don't know if I actually said that…" Danica tried to recall the exact words of their phone conversation the previous week. It was Paige who called him that, right? "Isn't that what you said?"

"It doesn't matter who gave him the nickname," Katrina insisted. "The only question I have is this: does the doctor live up to it?"

"To that nickname?"

Katrina rolled her eyes as if she had no time for wasted words. "Yes, that name."

Danica dipped her head, rolling her shoulder as her shirt shrugged off the side of it. "I don't know."

"Liar." Esmee shot a sly smile over the edge of her glass as she took a sip.

"You are," Katrina echoed. "I have a feeling you think this guy is hot."

With all this prodding and banter, any doubts Danica had about Dr. Urban were being pushed aside. "And what if he is?"

"Then I only have one thing to say to you, my friend." Katrina raised her drink, signaling the others to do the same. All four friends brought their glasses into raised formation between them. "You are going to have your future toasted. To the start of something between Danica and Dr. McHottie!"

Danica rolled her eyes as the girls clinked their nearly-downed mocktails one final time. The final toast put a temporary stop to their teasing but only revved the uncertainty within her for how she would handle seeing Grady again.

~*~

Spectacle Optique's front windows shone in the white-hot morning light. Grady opened the building, ready for another work week—and ready to shore-up the front displays. A cardboard sun hung in the corner of one window as fake waves curled in blue construction paper at the bottom. Upturned boxes covered with brown mailing paper held a small display of eyewear with a plastic pail and a sandcastle mold punctuating the scene to suggest a beach theme.

It was simple yet seasonal, and Grady was glad for Samantha's lead in being the one to envision and execute the office's changing window displays. If it were up to him, he'd simply hang a sign, maybe add a silk plant, and be done with the whole business of street view decorating. But that wasn't how small businesses handled the change of seasons in Seguin. A couple hours inland from the Gulf of Mexico coastline, businesses decorated with beach themes as aggressively as they did patriotic displays for July Fourth or springtime bloom displays approaching summer. Those, so far, were what Samantha had done, though more was coming and expected throughout the year.

Samantha arrived steps behind him, and he held aside the door to usher her inside.

"Morning, Samantha," Grady greeted.

"Morning, Dr. Urban." On the same wavelength, she pointed to the window display. "You know, I've been thinking it's about time to change these."

"Not a bad idea." Grady did think the construction paper waves were looking a little tired and sun-bleached anyway. "Do you have any thoughts about the next display?"

Samantha flicked on the lights and punched the wall thermostat lower, readying the waiting room. "We're heading into September, and we didn't do anything for a back-to-school theme. So I was thinking maybe something celebrating the start of school instead."

"Sure." Grady could get on board with that.

"Since I'm going to the elementary school Friday for the DEAR program, I thought—"

"About that." Grady snapped his fingers in realization. "I meant to tell you."

"What's that?" She spun to face him.

He had meant to address this plan with her—and the other employees—last week. But the moment he walked back into the office on Friday, it had been hit with a flurry of responsibilities. The mentorship schedule slid from his radar, until this moment. "I know we were going to take turns for the DEAR program, but I've kind of gotten myself into a commitment with Alexis."

"The girl from the program?" Samantha beamed with the pride of a parent. "Are you liking it?"

"Very much." That was the truth of it, and Grady smiled as he said the words. Alexis was such a doll, and seeing Mrs. Livingston's commitment to the program on a weekly basis was so inspiring. In a short time, he already felt like that classroom and that desk was where he needed to be week to week. "I didn't realize I'd enjoy it as much as I do."

"That's great." Samantha's words weren't forced in the least. "I'm happy that's the case."

"Me too." Grady thought about the supportive atmosphere in the classroom, adding, "It's just that these kids need extra help, and it seems like having an exact routine week to week is the best way to make progress." He added that he knew anyone could help, "but I didn't have the heart to tell Alexis that I wouldn't be coming this week."

"Say no more." Samantha raised a hand. "I completely understand."

"Do you think you can hold down the fort if I slip away again this Friday?"

Samantha gave a measure of assurance that spoke to why he hired her in the first place. "Absolutely." Grady thanked her, but not before Samantha made one request of him. "Do you think you can help with getting something for the window display? Maybe from the kids?"

"What do you have in mind?"

"Something school spirited. Maybe with the school colors and the mascot image. We can scrap those boxes and replace them with stacks of books." She stepped closer to the display window, now considering it more carefully from the inside of the building looking out. "Put new frames and cases on the top of each. Lean a small chalkboard against this side, some pom-poms draped in this corner for fun." She gestured like a designer explaining a new room concept. "Or if you can get your hands on some posters or flyers from the school, maybe we could string them across the top of the window in a cute display. I have some vintage wooden clothespins at home that would work."

Grady was getting more on board with this vision than he suspected. "I really like that idea."

"Good!" Samantha reached her hand to the edge where the cardboard sun hung and tapped it as it swayed. "It's about time to say good-bye to this anyway."

Samantha's vision had inspired one of Grady's own. "But what if we took it one step further?"

She cocked her head in consideration. "How's that?"

"What if we asked the kids to create art to display instead of school posters?" Grady flashed to Alexis, Owen, and the other children of the DEAR program. An art project might really give them a chance to shine.

Samantha snapped her fingers. "Love that idea!"

"I'll ask on Friday."

"I'll make an information sheet explaining how we'll use the art. I'll put our address and phone number on it. You can take it to Mrs. Livingston and see if she needs anything for parents to read or sign or if she just wants to let the kids do it optionally."

"Sounds great." This impromptu idea was already making him more involved in the window display aspect of his business than he had been in any months prior. Samantha had taken the lead because she really seemed to enjoy it, and now Grady was realizing how this little bit of a creative outlet could be fun too, especially in partnership with the community. "The kids will really like this."

"And I think they'll be proud to have their work

displayed." Samantha edged Grady with a shoulder bump. "Might even drive in a few new clients if their parents or grandparents come by to see the windows."

Advertising and outreach needed his vigilance, yet Grady still was uncomfortable with how to make big decisions there. Growth, to some extent, needed to be grassroots, though creating a pipeline of customers this first year was something he knew he needed to proactively do. "New customers would be a good bonus."

"It's settled then." Samantha turned from the window to walk to the reception area. "I'll make a flyer and work on getting everything else for the window. You go on Friday, and we can add the art finishing touches later."

"Sounds like a plan." Grady's Monday was already shaping up well. He looked once more to Samantha, who held none of the sadness that Iris had hinted would be the case from her boyfriend breakup last week. Was it the two days off? Was it a Monday reset? Even after Iris revealed Samantha's breakup to him last week, he avoided saying anything so as not to rock the boat with either of them. Iris seemed all too interested in getting involved anyway, which continued to tug on Grady in an odd way. That line between personal lives and professional ones was still grayed. As the boss, he needed to run a tight ship, yet he wanted his employees to be comfortable, and he knew they had lives too.

Yet Iris was concerned enough about Samantha to suggest that Grady do something, so perhaps he should.

Samantha rounded the corner to her desk, readying herself at the reception area. She pulled back her chair, punched the power on her computer station, and glanced to the phone. Before she had time to pick it up to check messages, Grady decided this was his opportunity. "Samantha, are you doing OK since, um..." He stepped closer toward her, the reception counter a buffer between them. "Since your breakup last week?" Grady drew a breath and waited for her response.

But she scrunched her eyebrows and furrowed her forehead. "Why wouldn't I be?"

Iris's recommendation for sympathy flowers flashed in his mind's eye as he searched for words. "I just thought you might be a little upset."

Samantha huffed in quiet defiance, taking a seat in her chair. "That loser is the one who's upset, not me. I'm better off." She didn't seem to hold the look of a scorned girlfriend, pining for a lost relationship. "I'm the one who ended it, and I'm glad I did."

"You ended it?" Grady couldn't even think of her boyfriend's name at the moment. The surprise of her being the enactor was enough to cloud that for him. Hadn't Iris said Samantha had been dumped? Or if she hadn't said it, hadn't she suggested it? That's what Grady thought, but Samantha's reaction spoke to the opposite of that. How could he have gotten this so wrong?

"I needed to end it. And I'm happy about it. Best thing for us both," Samantha affirmed with the confidence of someone far from the depths of relationship doldrums.

Had Grady taken Iris's advice and sent flowers, what message would that have sent? He silently thanked his interior compass for directing him to not follow Iris. "Can I ask one more thing?" He didn't want to push, yet he needed to know.

Samantha opened the office's appointment calendar, smoothing the page to the start of a new week. "Sure. Shoot."

"Did you tell Iris that you'd been dumped?"

Samantha looked up from the calendar, shifting in her seat with an expression of confusion, as if she were on a hidden camera show. "No. Why?"

No reason. But Grady couldn't say that. Not at this point. He settled instead on a half-truth that he hoped would be sensitive to them both. "I think she was just worried about you last week. Maybe she sensed something was going on?"

"The only thing going on,"—she kept her voice low even though it was still just the two of them—"is that Iris has heart eyes for you."

That admission punched Grady harder than realizing Samantha's truth. The last thing he needed was anyone, especially another employee, thinking there was reason to worry about impropriety.

"She's young." Samantha waved her hand as if dismissing any worry. She wasn't much older than Iris but seemed a world away in maturity, at least in this moment. "She'll realize one day that starting drama isn't all it's cracked up to be." She gave a carefully worded caution to Grady. "Just remember that she's fragile, lacks a little confidence sometimes, and wants to please people. You especially. She'll get over her crush on you the minute someone else catches her eye."

Samantha was perceptive, yet honesty aside, this talk was a little too close for Grady's comfort.

"Some women fall hard," she added. "That's all I'm going to say." She picked up the receiver of the office phone, signaling an end to their conversation as she begun the duties of her work week.

Yet something about those words made Grady's mind flash. Perhaps it was her word choice, for though their conversation had been about Iris, another woman edged into Grady's thought in a burned image. And it wasn't Iris falling.

It was Danica Lara, a woman who fell in his presence for an entirely different reason. And for some reason Grady couldn't identify, he had a hard time halting the long-dormant feeling of falling as well.

Falling into something he couldn't see.

Falling into something he didn't know he wanted.

But maybe he did.

FOURTEEN

A weekend girls' night and a busy work week were enough to reset Danica and push Cameron's reprimand far from her mind.

Almost.

Her Friday with Paige, Katrina, and Esmee had been a sunny distraction from the low-hanging cloud that was her boss's written warning. Being with her friends helped her put the setback in perspective. She wasn't a bad employee; she just needed to focus exclusively on work during work hours.

So she did that. All week, the result of Cameron's reprimand was that it loomed near enough that it cemented Danica into her best behavior, which was likely her supervisor's intent all along.

At the appraisal district, Danica arrived early. She stayed a few minutes late, just in case the time clock ran slow. She double checked her watch to bookend her lunch break with a prompt beginning and end. And, most importantly, she avoided any use of her personal cell phone during work hours.

The habit of doing that was hard to break, but she had phoned Barry on Sunday with a firm "Do not call me at work" warning. "And don't even think about coming by the office." Her reliable county paycheck took precedence over the unsure return of the Cinnamon Ridge Estates venture. Barry continued to make optimistic promises of a heavy financial return, but Danica would only believe it when she saw it.

And so far, she hadn't seen it.

What she did see with clarity was her Friday DEAR time commitment, a slice of volunteerism that broke up the lassitude of her work week. It was the one excused outing to which Cameron had already committed, so she couldn't dock her for going or coming, as long as she did so during the expected time.

The commitment gave Danica something to which she could look forward, and she was happy to go to a place where she was getting used to the same faces from week to week. She was developing familiarity with the other volunteers, waving to a couple of them she saw throughout the week at the grocery store or on an evening errand. And, of course, there were the special plans she had with one volunteer in particular, the upcoming River Walk Labor Day Arts and Crafts Show that was approaching on Saturday. Grady hadn't clarified their exact San Antonio agenda as far as transportation and timing, but she suspected they could do that without much fuss on Friday. But she wasn't going to make a motion toward that during DEAR time. Just as she was committing to work during work time, she held the same commitment to her assigned student during DEAR time.

She found herself turning over in her mind ways to help Owen, remaining hopeful for progress with him. She had no firm plan other than to stay the course. He was a kid whom she sensed would respond only after stability was established and just showing up week to week was going to help with that.

Even though she didn't see leaps and bounds improvement yet with Owen, Mrs. Livingston insisted all the children in the program benefited from the routine. "Progress is sometimes hard to measure." Danica appreciated Mrs. Livingston's words, even though educators like her were beholden to the metrics of standardized testing and numerical classroom grades. Still, there was a lot of education that could take place outside of those boundaries.

Arriving at SES, Danica felt a spring in her step as she navigated to Mrs. Livingston's classroom. When she arrived, Grady was already seated, waiting for Alexis and the rest of the children to arrive.

He waved and wished her a good morning as she took her seat. "Good morning," she returned.

Grady slid a flyer across the table toward her. "Tell me what you think."

She picked up the bright yellow printout and held it at an angle as she read it through her glasses. "An art display option for the kids? Gallery Optique?" She raised an eyebrow. "So you're turning your office window into a gallery for the kids?"

"Why not?" His interior enthusiasm reflected in his exterior countenance, a wide grin spanning ear to ear.

Danica couldn't help but smile back at the doctor's extra layer of involvement with the kids. "Sounds like a fun idea."

"I asked Mrs. Livingston about it earlier in the week, and she shared the idea with the art teacher." Grady accepted the printout as Danica handed it back to him. "She said she'll work with the DEAR kids during their art hour to help them plan something for the window, something that promotes reading and literacy so there's a connection to this program." Grady seemed quite pleased with himself.

"I'm impressed."

"I am too." He said how much fun it would be to see the kids' work in the window, adding, "It will give them a sense of accomplishment, too."

"Win-win." Danica saw the benefits of a partnership. "It might even net a few more volunteers for the program. If you put the DEAR letters in one corner of the window or add something in the office about the program, I'm sure Mrs. Livingston would like that."

"Great idea!" Grady added, "For someone who's new here, I must admit I didn't expect all of this."

"What do you mean?" Danica kicked her purse a bit further under the table before she crossed her feet at the ankles, settling in to hear more.

"It's been really wonderful." He looked around the room, contentment reflected in his face. "This community impresses me. The people, the teachers here at the school, the kids. I just want to be a part of that, you know?"

"You are." Every citizen was, but a business owner held a role unique to others. "You're charged with a whole office, one that helps people." She tapped the corner of her glasses as she reminded him, "You helped me."

"I know. And I don't want to forget that." He reiterated a simple and admirable wish. "I want to do my part. That's all."

Pairs of footfalls against tile and a morning greeting from Mrs. Livingston halted their conversation. The attention of each volunteer was called to the classroom door as the teacher heralded the arrival of the kids. To Danica's surprise, Owen led the line.

And there was a spring in his step unlike Danica had seen.

He held his head upright, shoulders not slumped as had been the case when he walked in previous weeks. His crude scar still cut across his forehead, yet Danica's eyes were drawn away from it as she couldn't help but sense something akin to enthusiasm in the way he approached.

She expected Owen to sit next to her in silent reluctance as he had done in the past. But something was different. Instead of being met with tight lips, the third grader surprised by opening his mouth first. "We get to draw today."

"We do?" Since Mrs. Livingston was out of the room when Danica arrived, and since there were no written instructions for the volunteers on the tables, she wasn't sure about the day's agenda.

"After we read, we get to do a drawing that might be displayed in a gallery." Owen leaned into Danica to share the whisper of words, which held the promise of opportunity of someone whom had never had anything close to this ever offered.

"That's cool." Danica smiled knowingly.

The promise of opportunity was thanks to Grady. And as she glanced his direction, she hoped he could read the appreciation in her eyes for the gifts he was giving Owen and all the children.

~*~

Grady was no expert when it came to understanding children. He cared for a few in his office, but since he didn't specialize in pediatric optometry, he didn't have a large client base of school-age children.

He always considered himself awkward around children because he grew up in the shadow of parents who wanted more than they had. His well-to-do father and mother built a four-bedroom house and planned to fill it with love, laughter, and little ones. But his mother was unable to have more children after giving birth to Grady, making him an only child by default.

Two bedrooms which were meant for future siblings held unfulfilled hope instead. Closets built for children's clothes went unused. Space that was supposed to hold cribs and then toddler beds never did. Their emptiness spoke to the never-born.

When Grady entered elementary school, he understood the reality in which his parents lived. They were a family of three, and that's all they would be.

So Grady learned to make friends, but much of his

life was spent alone.

There was love in his house, sometimes laughter—
but no more little ones as planned.

Grady's time alone in imaginative play allowed
him plenty of opportunity to explore the world he saw
in lush colors, bright contrasts, and striking displays.
But he needed help seeing with sharpness, so when he
had his first optometry appointment as a teen and was
fitted with glasses, he became fascinated with the field.
His love affair with understanding sight began.

But discovery was not without disappointment.

Board games with colored squares that looked the
same to other kids hadn't always looked that way to
Grady. Video games, intense enough before he wore
glasses, now seemed too intense for him to enjoy. He
often wanted to wear sunglasses just to mute the world
around him, but rather than understanding that his
eyes sometimes needed a break, classmates poked fun
at him for trying too hard to look cool.

But adjusting to sight was Grady's reality.

So as he sat next to Alexis, a sweet girl but one
who struggled with the concept of reading that most of
her peers had mastered well enough for their ages, he
understood a sliver of her experience. She was in
DEAR because she needed assistance. And whether
that was because she was behind the expected curve or
because it was the result of something genetically
unique about her that had not yet been diagnosed,
Grady could only wonder. Yet the best he could do for
her was make her feel accepted and important and
normal during DEAR time.

So that's what he did.

He stayed focused with Alexis on their task. He made sure to ask her questions about their activity and listen meaningfully as she answered. When she didn't want to answer, he respected her shyness. And he made sure to give her, as Mrs. Livingston had encouraged all the mentors to do, gentle praise as she conquered new words and pushed through challenging pronunciations.

"Great job, Alexis!" He cheered, and he meant it.

He knew what it was like to struggle with something, and he realized the barriers it put between him and others long ago. That life as an only child—and as one with glasses—had made him a bit different than others.

Yet the world was full of differences.

Akin to a color scale, those differences created a spectrum of beauty. Grady always tried to remember that.

In much the same way as he had come to accept difference, Grady wanted Alexis to know there was no shame in hers. Learning at her own pace was just fine, which was partly what prompted his use of a book prescription last week. According to Mrs. Livingston, all the other kids were envious, so this week, he brought the pad to write every one of the children a prescription that they could take home. Securing it to the fridge, taping it to a bedroom mirror, or just folding it into a backpack would be, he hoped, a positive reminder for each child to practice reading.

Now just three weeks into the DEAR routine, he

was realizing he had something unique to offer. He hadn't previously considered it, but using his skills in this way was a type of advocacy. And all children needed advocates.

Alexis seemed to be making progress. As they read an assigned book and then transitioned into the start of the art project they would develop further with the guidance of their art teacher, Grady was glad he had offered the display window idea to Mrs. Livingston as well. He liked seeing the children's enthusiasm for creating something new, and seeing the way Alexis chose colors and applied them to a page fired up his receptors, which would also get plenty of visual stimulation at the following day's art show.

He glanced to Danica, where Owen was more engaged than Grady had ever seen him. He had the outline drawing of a masterpiece for which only he knew the final shape. Still, he was pointing and chattering with Danica as she passed various crayons his way. This was the most animated he had seen the boy and the most contented he had seen Danica.

Like the pictures the children created, the whole scene was taking shape. Kids worked hard, and volunteers played their parts. The school/community partnership was a stroke of genius.

Grady just hoped the blank canvas of his Saturday with Danica would take shape with as much natural progression and easy effort as this day.

At the end of DEAR time, every student had an impressive start on a literacy-inspired drawing that they would have one week to complete. Mrs.

Livingston gathered the students a few minutes early so they could all deliver their works-in-progress to the art teacher's class before heading back to their homerooms. "Children, let's give Dr. Urban a round of applause for donating the window gallery to display all of your work!" The children burst into happy claps from their positions in line, balancing their proud pieces of paper under the safety of elbows, between knees, or on the tops of their heads as they did. Their grins and giggles lit Grady from the inside.

"It really was a great idea." Danica leaned toward him. Some of the other volunteers followed suite in offering their appreciation, saying how the kids opened up in new ways and how the introduction of something that would be on display made them take today's lesson much more seriously.

"Who would have guessed?" Grady was glad. "I really just wanted a nice display window at the office," he joked.

"Small actions can have big effects." Danica called Grady on his martyrdom downplaying.

"I'll remember that," he assured her.

"Now, Dr. Urban," Mrs. Livingston called to him and motioned for him to stand. "Is it time for the kids to receive their prescriptions?"

"Yes." He looked to Danica whose eyes looked like espresso pods.

"What are you doing?" she mouthed.

Grady lifted the pad and paper from his shirt pocket without answering.

The kids lined up with gusto.

As he finished the last prescription and Mrs. Livingston gathered the children back into line formation, Danica offered her appraisal. "Incredible."

"It's a notepad. I could pretty much write a made-up prescription for anything," he whispered as the kids left the room.

"You could." She uncrossed her arms. "But you chose to do something special. Something meaningful."

"You would do the same."

Danica, by virtue of being a mentor in the first place, was showing her giving side. Selflessness and a desire to help others was attractive to Grady.

"I don't have a prescription pad. But kudos to you for now having two home run ideas today." She held up a V-shape with her fingers.

"Let's hope that luck continues through the weekend." He winked her way. "For San Antonio?"

Danica's mind must have already been there because she transitioned to the logistics of the day. "About that. Are we going to talk about how that's going to work?"

Grady wasn't sure, as this was new territory for him. "I've never been to the River Walk, but I'm happy to drive."

"That's fine by me. I can navigate."

So far, so good. This was effortless.

But was another home run idea too much to hope for?

Danica stood and grabbed her purse. Still, a bit of planning needed to be finalized. "What do you think of an early start?"

"How early?" he asked.

Danica suggested eight o'clock, which was just like a normal workday for either of them anyway.

"That's not early to me."

"But it's a Saturday. I don't want to impose." Was it that? Or did she want to maximize their time together? The closer they got to their planned outing, the less Grady knew how to read it. And for a literacy mentor who just finished instructing the very task of reading, that realization unnerved him more than blurred vision.

FIFTEEN

San Antonio strummed with the rhythm of pedestrians and their purse strings for the annual River Walk Labor Day Arts and Crafts Show. Spring-fed waterways that tumbled toward the Guadalupe River created the centerpiece of the River Walk. Intricate stone retaining walls, meandering walkways, and arched bridges framed the space in old-world style. Yet Texas traditions and character shone through in the music, cuisine, and cultural artistry that could be enjoyed on either side of the river that bisected the heart of the city.

Danica had always enjoyed San Antonio, and she never tired of this downtown area. Riverfront patios, hotels, and restaurant seating spilled into every available space, making even a short distance worth the walk. Strolling was her favorite thing to do in this gorgeous oasis.

When she got tired, she'd hail one of many riverboat taxis that glided across the water. All it took was a quick signal. The captain would pull the open-air vessel next to the walkway to pick up or deposit passengers so they could make new discoveries along the miles and miles of networked waterfront.

"I'm surprised you've never been to downtown."

Danica suggested a parking garage for Grady, and she led the way onto Commerce Street that, once they descended the steps below street level, would put them squarely in line with the River Walk.

"I've been through downtown, but that's about it." Grady admitted he had never stopped anywhere off the interstate. "Though I have seen plenty of Spurs games on television."

Seeing basketball broadcasts from San Antonio was one thing, but it was no substitute for visiting the area. "But never Paseo Del Rio?" Danica used crisp pronunciation.

"Rio being . . ."

"River." Danica said it with such simplicity that Grady bristled at his ignorance. "There's nothing to be ashamed of there. Now you know your first Spanish word."

"So Paseo Del Rio," —Grady articulated each word—"means…"

"You tell me," Danica teased.

"Let's see. What sounds logical?" Grady placed his hand at the small of Danica's back to guide her along stone steps. "Is it pass? Pass along the river?"

"Not a bad first guess. You're getting warmer."

"City?" He tried again, leaning close to her shoulder so she wasn't out of earshot as they descended. Danica smelled his cologne, something smoky yet sweet. The sensation was as alluring as his proximity to her.

"That's cuidad," she called over her shoulder, a strand of her hair lifting in the wind and tempting the closure of distance between them. "Try again. Think of what we're doing. Right now."

Grady looked to his feet. "Walking?"

"Bingo!" She spun around as she stepped off the bottom stair, turning to him so fast he nearly rammed into her. "Paseo Del Rio means 'river walk' in Spanish." She congratulated him with a playful high-five.

Grady put his hands on her shoulders, making heavy eye contact before pivoting her back in the direction they were headed. "If we don't keep moving, we're going to create a river jam."

"I don't know that Spanish word," she teased. "But I'm glad I could teach the doctor some new skills."

Grady fell into step next to her, walking companionably. "This is San Antonio?" he marveled. "From this viewpoint, it's not at all like the metropolitan downtown I expected."

"Oh, this is San Antonio." Danica beamed. "I'm glad to introduce you to all this." She raised her hand in presentation over the space, as if she were Grady's own private tour guide. Even though they were a short drive from Seguin, the atmosphere felt a world away.

"It's nice to loosen up a bit. I've been needing to get out of the office."

"And a school classroom doesn't count?"

"Definitely not. This is the casual escape I needed."

They pointed toward sights that caught their eyes, commented on unique architecture, and shared impressions of the areas they passed. They didn't need a map, and they didn't need a plan. Walking the river—just as the name suggested—was all they needed to do.

"And you know where we're going?"

"I know exactly where we're going," Danica insisted. Between the river, the water taxis, the storefronts, the hidden green spaces, and all the hustle and bustle of people just like them exploring the space, there were sights and colors aplenty. But heading in a single direction and taking it slow gave them time to savor everything they encountered. "The vendors are this way."

Between the Alamo Street Bridge and the River Center Mall, rows of vendors splayed before them. Turning a corner from one, there was another and another and another. Paintings, sculptures, rugs, jewelry, yard art, and all other manners of crafts provided feasts for the eyes and temptations for the wallet.

"I don't even know where to look."

"We'll take it slow."

"Thank you." Grady's hand brushed the top of Danica's, sending a shiver of longing through her.

Being in his company felt safe.

Secure.

And slightly sensual.

As quickly, though, as the motion happened, the spell broke as he gestured to his right. "So these people aren't just exhibiting this stuff?"

"Most are artisans." Danica nodded toward a table

full of clay jars and figurines, hand-painted in splendid designs. "That's what's so fun about this. Getting to see creations up close and getting to speak with the people who created them." She tucked a flyaway strand of hair behind her ear as she leaned over to examine a piece.

Grady shadowed her as she stopped to appreciate some pottery. As she did, the exhibitor struck up a conversation, but it wasn't in English.

Danica switched effortlessly into Spanish, her words confident and strong. She and the vendor exchanged pleasantries about the day, and then she pointed to a row of painted pots, all festooned with flowers but each with an individualized design. "¿Cuánto cuesta?"

"Diaz."

Danica turned to Grady. "Ten dollars. That's a good price."

"That's all?"

The exhibitor held up one pot that was as unique as a snowflake, turned it over to the bottom, and pointed to the initials. "Me," she said to Grady.

"Very nice." He complimented the work, and even though his words were simple, Danica could tell he meant them.

The vendor artist smiled in kind. "Mucho bueno."

Grady repeated the words, much to Danica's delight. "You'll be speaking with fluency in no time."

"I don't know about that." He chuckled.

Danica reached for a clay pot no bigger than a baseball. A bright yellow flower adorned the natural red clay of the material. Sleek black outlining finished the edged. "It's cute." She held it level, turning it to admire the way the petals curved. "I think I'll use it at my desk for paper clips. What do you think?"

"I think you selected a winner." He lowered his voice, whispering to her, "And you got a bargain."

The tenderness and support of Grady's quiet words settled into her, a feeling she wanted to experience more and more.

She passed her selection back to the woman, who wrapped it before accepting Danica's cash. She thanked the vendor, tucked her purchase into a zippered pouch of her purse, and held out her hand as Grady grasped it, heading into a day full of promise.

But as they strolled hand in hand, Danica wondering if she was thinking straight. She extended an automatic gesture to Grady that she didn't even see coming. But once her hand closed the gap between them, Grady latched onto it, lacing his fingers into hers as if the act were the most natural gesture in the world.

So Danica and Grady continued to walk hand in hand, and to any casual observer, their link might as well have been.

Wrist to wrist, palm on palm, and fingers in between fingers, not a hint of air could have passed through their contact. Grady's skin was warm, and a tingle of electricity swirled where they touched. Close to him, she could smell and experience his distinctness. How long had it been since she had held hands with a man?

Too long.

As she allowed the comfort of his presence to settle into her, her nervous surprise turned into something much more manageable. She had been averting her eyes to the exhibitors, but summoning courage, she turned to look at Grady as they stepped in tune together with slow, measured steps as if they didn't have a care in the world.

And when he looked back at her, it was like she didn't.

Tingling from her hand moved through her chest and wrapped close to her heart. Her voice caught in her throat. Unable to speak—or perhaps afraid to for fear of rocking the moment—she moved her fingers in such a way that resulted in a gentle hand squeeze against Grady's.

He squeezed back, and his smile was as noticeable as their interlocked grasp.

"I didn't expect this either." He spoke first, his head angling toward hers as if he were going to tell a joke. But instead of breaking the ice with humor, he addressed what Danica was thinking.

The honesty of his comment jolted Danica where she needed it. She cleared her throat of a few syllables, still beside herself. But no actual words came.

"If it's OK with you," Grady's voice was gentle, "I'd like to keep this going for as long as you'll let us."

A relationship?

Danica didn't know what she wanted. She didn't know what she was doing.

But she did know that this felt good. Holding this man's hand. Walking beside him. And when she couldn't figure out much else, at least knowing those things was a step in the right direction.

She smiled, keeping her body upright though it wanted to curl into itself from so much stimulation that had long been dormant. Keep it together. Be an adult. She needed a quick pep talk to tell herself she wasn't a teenager, though the freshness of feeling made her body think it so.

"I like where this is going," she admitted.

"Good." Grady smiled.

Around them, the scene buzzed and hummed with activity. Tables, tents, and other creative displays unfolded into their view one right after the other. Some had large signs or banners identifying their name or products. Others let their art speak for itself. Items were displayed in all kinds of ways. Most had plenty of products immediately for purchase, though some had booklets with more information or a selection of photographs to aid people in making special orders. Some even had credit card paying options and signs about the availability to ship products worldwide.

Danica liked the single entrepreneurs the best, the ones without fancy announcements or means. There was beauty in a lone artist standing next to his or her work, waiting for the opportunity to catch the eye of some passersby and speak about it.

"Look at that." Danica slowed her steps in front of a vendor whose large canvases of abstract art caught her eye. "What do you think of these?"

"I didn't think I liked modern art. But these I do," he added quickly. "I want to see more of them."

Grady's eyes flashed with focus as he turned into the vendor's u-shaped display. "Good morning," he nodded to the woman seated behind a table at an easel.

"Good morning." She suspended her brush stoke just long enough for a quick acknowledgement. "Look around," she instructed. "Let me know if you have questions." She leaned into her canvas again, her attention on her work.

Danica and Grady had the whole makeshift outdoor gallery of this woman's art to themselves. Each piece had a similar style, yet the colors and exact shapes were wildly different. At a distance, every painted canvas looked like a giant piece of graph paper with colored squares in ombre patterns. Geometric shapes, mostly spheres, were the focal point, with some looking like suns, others like moons, still others like ethereal orbs with origins Danica couldn't identify. Yet she stared, taking in their beauty. "These are incredible. The colors of them all..." She trailed as sight enjoyed what her mouth couldn't articulate.

"I know what you mean." Grady still held fast to her hand. "Look at this one with me." He directed her to a horizontal canvas in shades of blue with four tangerine spheres that looked like the phases of the sun. "Tell me what you see."

They stood side by side linked together as if they were using both sets of eyes to make sense of what they saw. There was something sensual about the way they stood, yet there was a calmness over Danica that made her comfortable in the moment, happy to be where she was with who she was. They shared complete captivation together.

If she could have bottled that moment, she would have.

After finding words in her mind, she drew a breath to answer Grady's question. "Cobalt and indigo. Sapphire, teal, turquoise." She rattled the color names of as many shades of blue she knew.

"I see those too," Grady whispered, still as transfixed as Danica.

"Sky colors and marine colors and hues I don't even know how to name." One color family was so varied that Danica couldn't help but continue to stare.

And, as far as she sensed, Grady was content to do the same.

The gridding of squares that comprised the background was so exact. Each square had to have been the same dimensions as the ones that surrounded it. Yet up close, Danica could see layers of paint that made the edges of some squares stand out more than others. From far away, the painting had one look. Up close, it was completely different. "How does she do that?" Danica's question for the artist was so quiet that she didn't expect a response. Nor did she get one. Instead, Grady asked another question. "And the circles? Tell me what you see in those?"

Those required deeper concentration. They had a similar layering upon layering of paint, so much that each looked three dimensional, suspended as if weightless atop the canvas. To the naked eye, the four circles also appeared to be gridded in exact proportions and placement, the four of them in concert together as if forming the edges of the squares below them. But they were much larger that Danica wondered if that's where the artist intended the real mystery to be. The base of the spheres was tangerine in color, but an incredible array of hues could be seen up close, with reds and yellows licking the surface to create a dazzling display. "I see orange, but so many shades that they look fiery and fruity all at the same time."

As soon as Danica heard her own words, she realized how ridiculous and pedestrian they sounded. But Grady didn't laugh. Not even close to it. He stayed, held onto her, and let her experience the joy of seeing and being part of art that transfixed them both into a place she had never before been. And from which she never wanted to leave.

Sixteen

Grady wasn't sure if he was shopping for office art or playing the role of a couple with Danica as they wandered together through the River Walk. Until the moment of physical contact with Danica's hand in his, he hadn't realized how good that simple act of coupledom could feel. It wasn't forced, yet it wasn't desperate. The spontaneity caught him off guard, but there was a calmness in the way they settled together. Physical contact with this woman by his side seemed to seal an emotional fault line that existed within him. The crack that made him scared of a future relationship was non-existent in these moments with Danica.

Had he been that focused on the office? Had he ignored emotions that he should have understood?

Grady wasn't sure how to answer questions that he asked himself, but he was certain that he wanted to continue in the company of Danica. Being next to her — and being with her — happened on autopilot.

Previous relationships always took work and planning. To even arrive at the point of hand holding, Grady had always considered the moment and then waited for a sign or opportunity. He had to think about his actions. It was laborious.

But being with Danica wasn't work. It was

effortless.

And as he asked her what she saw in the paintings, her answers made him enjoy what he saw too. He was able to share the moment with her and for that sliver of time, he was simply a man holding the hand of a woman enjoying the beauty of what was before them.

Without taking his eyes from the painting, Grady considered the length and width. He couldn't be sure, and he hadn't taken measurements for the space. But it looked about the right size. Surely, it could work. If it had half the effect on other optometry patients as it was having on him, it would be an eye-catching piece. There was no question in Grady's mind. "I need this painting for the office."

Danica didn't take her eyes from the canvas as he spoke, but she leaned her head onto his shoulder. Soft pressure with softly spoken words of encouragement for the purchase was a moment that lit all of his senses on fire.

Maybe Grady should have been more level-headed. Maybe he should have considered his next move.

But he didn't.

He simply acted on what his emotion told him to do.

He unlocked his hand from Danica's and reached up to cup her cheek, directing her gaze to his. He bent his head toward her and leaned down for a kiss that held surprise for them both.

Danica's smooth lips met Grady's, their touch

intimate yet sweet. Grady closed his eyes to savor the moment.

Shared affection between them had grown from comfortable interactions to this pinnacle of sensual contact. His mouth caressed hers, a gentle and meaningful exchange that, like the canvas before them, was deceptively simple yet layered in meaning.

Grady pulled back only when his lips had expressed what they needed to share. Opening his eyes, he saw Danica in a way his body had understood as his mind was just beginning to make sense of it all.

Maybe he should listen less to his brain and more to his heart. He bit his lip as he pulled back, biting against the desire to express more to her. This one kiss would be enough.

For now.

~*~

First the hand holding.

Then the head-against-shoulder contact.

Now a kiss.

The current of Danica's emotion moved faster than the spring-fed river whose bank they paralleled. Her stomach flip-flopped as fluttering tickled her throat, momentarily making her mute.

Not that she had anything to say anyway.

As Grady pulled his lips from hers, she opened her eyes to see her own reflection in the lenses of his glasses. Looking beyond the outline of her face, she bore deeper to see his eyes, slicing through their veneer and sensing their longing. This wasn't just a kiss of curiosity. Though coated with familiarity, it had something more at its core.

Mere inches away, they shared the silence as they both processed what had happened.

Danica wanted Grady to be the first to speak because her tongue was tied. Sensations rushed, but words wouldn't form.

If it were the same for him, she had no way of knowing.

He dropped his hand, letting it fall into her fingers. Lacing them again into one another, he held her with a comforting touch that made her squeeze his grip in reply.

Sometimes, no words were best.

As they recovered from the mutual shock of a kiss that they both wanted and seemed to enjoy, Danica turned back to the painting, letting her breath slow as she refocused her attention. Looking again at the canvas, she tried to filter all of her emotion into interpreting the design. Simple yet grand, captivating and comforting, the finished product was a perfect resting place for her gaze.

Grady joined her in rediscovering the canvas with a second look. She held fast to his hand as he did, savoring this movement and their partnership of discovery.

Finally, Danica found her voice enough to broker the silence. "You said you have to have this for the office?"

"After what just happened," he lowered his voice

to a sensual whisper, "I insist on having it."

A leg-weakening thrill coursed through Danica, as the world seemed to tilt on its axis. His lips were so close to her ear that she could feel them move as he spoke, his warm breath reaching the tip and curling 'round and 'round to fill her mind with more sensory overload than it could stand. She lowered her head, as if a quick dip would shake off the blanket of Grady's sensuality. Instead, he stayed close, his presence wrapping her more tightly than before.

One kiss wasn't enough.

But short of hijacking this little corner of an exhibitor's display and claiming it as their own, a second kiss would have to wait.

Buying this painting, however, didn't.

"How much?" Danica didn't see a tag.

Grady angled to one side before spotting the piece of masking tape with its triple digit price. He pointed to it. "Right here."

Danica bent into him, getting a welcome second whiff of his clean, fresh aroma that she was starting to recognize as characteristic of him alone. She inhaled to capture the scent of him for a moment longer. Then, fueled by the sensation, she appraised the price being asked for the painting. "It's on the low side of what original art typically costs."

"I want to remember this." His eyes met hers again. "I didn't know this was possible with you, but I want this." Now, he wasn't just talking about the painting. "I won't push, but I'll take whatever you're willing to give."

Danica looked at him, and a sudden, childlike realization made her bring her hand to her mouth. It wasn't the reaction she planned, but the cute scene hit her, and she worked to cover an amused snicker.

Grady raised an eyebrow, his level of surprise in Danica matching her own. "What's so funny?"

Danica wanted to dismiss her slipup, and she waved her hand as if doing so would rewind the scene by just a few seconds.

No luck.

He dropped her hand and asked again. "What's so funny?"

Danica didn't want their contact to stop, and the moment his fingers left hers, she missed them. "Oh, please don't think I'm laughing at you," she hedged, not wanting him to assume she was doing so. "I'm really not laughing at—"

"Me?" Grady raised both eyebrows.

Yet her snickering broke through her smile, and she allowed herself to give in to a small choke of laughter. She pointed to her glasses with one hand and patted her chest with the other, an odd pantomime only she understood.

The corners of Grady's mouth started to turn upward. He took a wild guess. "Glasses?"

Danica made a hardline nod with her head. Summoning her voice, she admitted, "I've never kissed with glasses before."

Grady's cheeks reddened by a shade, and even though Danica couldn't see herself, she felt her own do the same. "And now you have."

The moment made her feel like a teenager. They exchanged fresh and flirty attention, all in a casual environment where one moment led to another. None of how they acted in the last ten minutes had been planned, yet it seemed to unfold naturally.

Maybe hand holding and a semi-public kiss should have made Danica self-conscious. But it had the opposite effect. It made her comfortable and confident, enough that she expressed how forward she was looking to the rest of their time together today.

"Me too." Grady kept breezy banter between them, yet he did manage to dish some sarcasm in her direction. "After all, this is my standard operating practice. Exam, prescription, and a kiss to get the girl." He ended with a wink.

Danica was a sucker for that move. She winked back. And she didn't even need to tell Grady in that moment that he already had her.

~*~

Grady enjoyed himself. The rest of the day unfolded in romantic perfection. After paying for the artwork they both loved and a sister piece in a smaller style but with the colors in reverse, Danica and Grady each grabbed a canvas and carried it back to the car, dodging pedestrians and meandering through clusters of crowds as they did. They laughed with each funny turn or quirky angle where they had to shift the canvas this way or that, contorting their bodies in exaggerated stretches to make each other laugh.

Once they reached the street level, Grady held the art high above his head like a makeshift umbrella as they crossed Commerce, shielding the sun above while colors cast through the canvas to rain shades of blue and orange across his blond hair. Danica laughed some more before following suit with his move, the two of them scurrying like thieves to beat the crosswalk sign as traffic honked in furry.

"Guess not everyone is happy about a downtown event." Grady let Danica step onto the curb first.

"This traffic?" Danica huffed. "This is nothing. San Antonio gets much worse."

Grady met Danica's pace and walked beside her before each brought their canvas to the side. They headed back into the parking garage, stowed the purchases in Grady's backseat, and turned to reverse their path once again into a further afternoon of fun.

"I'll know my way around here in no time," Grady avowed as they tracked their steps back to the River Walk.

"Good." Danica grabbed his hand, taking hold of his fingers that he longed to lace between hers. "Then you can be the leader next time we come."

Hand in hand once again, they went the opposite direction as before to see additional vendors. All kinds of media used by artists from varying skill levels was for sale. They stopped when one of them wanted to take a closer look. They compared prices and talked about which pieces would be perfect for people they knew. When they needed a break, they found a bench or stone ledge on which to sit where they could watch the water and rest.

Occasionally, music would drift on the breeze from its source within a restaurant or from a street performer they couldn't see. The beat would cause Grady to tap a foot in rhythm or Danica to bounce her hip a certain way. They fed off each other's energy, Grady discovering a kind of playfulness he didn't know he had.

At least not since starting his business.

His world had been awash in contracts and spreadsheets, schedules and reports. He had to plan for the first of the month, the end of the month, and every employee payday. There were elderly clients like Poppy who needed more attention than he anticipated. There were tough-to-crack clients like Skylar whom he wanted to help but wasn't sure he was doing his best to get through to.

Then there was the bottom line: profit and loss statements with income versus expenses to consider. He knew he wouldn't be in the black for a long time, but seeing Spectacle Optique in the red in these early months while he was still getting established was taking a toll on his psyche.

He was so wrapped up in getting a new business running that he had forgotten what it was like to enjoy simple pleasures. A stroll. People watching. The art scene in San Antonio. He needed this escape, and he needed the new outlook it was providing. Sure, he could have done this on his own like lots of other people he saw walking by themselves, but being in partnership was so much fun.

Who was he kidding? It wasn't just any partner who was making it fun. Danica was making this fun.

Her long, espresso hair lifted and lowered against the breeze, tangling with the frame of her glasses. She raised a delicate finger to sweep away the hair, shaking back her tresses from her shoulders and letting the sunlight set her face aglow. Her bright smile and laugh lines highlighted the parts of her at which Grady couldn't stop staring. The joy in her personality was contagious.

He wanted to stop for a photo or insist on a selfie of the two of them to capture the happiness he saw and experienced. But he also didn't want to cheapen the moment. He forced his mind to capture an impression, taking mental photographs all throughout the day.

They continued to stroll, seeing new sights around every turn. The arts and crafts were never-ending. So were the people who created them. Some artists were available to talk, and when they did, the two of them would gather as part of a small crowd of others to listen. Occasionally asking a question but being just as content to hear what others said, Grady stayed close to Danica's side. It seemed like they were comfortable in each other's company in a way that usually took longer to develop with another person.

Midafternoon, they stopped at a jewelry booth where Danica's attention was captured by sterling silver chains displayed against a black velvet background. "Those are pretty." She pointed to a collection of dainty chains that each held a single cut gemstone. The exhibitor was within earshot. "What are those?"

The man touched the side of one of the pendants, letting the facets in the gemstone play with the light. Dazzling streaks radiated from its crystalline center. "That's the state gemstone of Texas. Texas Topaz." He handed her a small card with an explanation.

Grady stood at Danica's back and looked over her shoulder to read about topaz and the spectrum of colors in which it could be found. Like any other gem, the artistry in the cut and the type of metal in which it was set gave it glamour.

The jeweler held up a couple of rough, uncut gemstones in white and honey colors for Danica's inspection. "I get mine out of Mason County. Between Austin and San Angelo."

"So they go from that," Grady pointed what looked like small rocks in his hand, "to that?"

"That's where I make the magic happen." The jeweler beamed with pride.

"Gorgeous," Danica breathed, her attention on one piece in particular. "May I?" She gestured to a necklace with a circular cut stone that wasn't the largest but shone more brilliantly than all the others.

Grady watched as she unhooked the clasp and let the pendant slide back and forth across the chain as she admired its sheen.

"That reminds me a little of the circles on the second painting we bought," he said.

Danica tilted her head in consideration. "It does." Smile lines lit her face.

"Do you want to try it on?" The jeweler adjusted a

display mirror in her direction.

"I'd like that."

She held each end of the necklace, but Grady intervened.

"Let me." He pinched the sterling silver clasp with one hand as he grasped around Danica's neck. "Hold your hair up for me, please?"

She gathered her hair with her fingers into a low ponytail and swept the strands upward in her palm, displaying a creamy neckline that begged for adornment. Grady set the chain against her skin and hinged the clasp, taking his time to enjoy the intimacy at seeing a sliver of skin he hadn't yet seen until this moment.

Danica's skin prickled against Grady's touch, light bumps dotting the surface that showed the spot he touched was slightly ticklish.

"Done," he announced, releasing his hands so Danica could do the same with her hair. But he stayed close, sneaking a peek in the mirror at her reflection as she saw herself wearing the necklace for the first time. "Stunning."

She brushed the pad of her finger against the pendant. "It is beautiful."

Grady leaned into her ear. "I wasn't just talking about the necklace."

She played coy—and wore the look well.

"I want to get this for you." It was as much a chance for him to show appreciation for the day as it was for Danica to have something that absolutely belonged on her. "No question, that necklace was made for you."

"It's too much," she dismissed, even though neither of them knew the price. She averted her gaze, but Grady drew her attention back to the mirror by cupping her cheek as he had done when they kissed.

"Do you like it?"

"Yes."

"Then let me do this."

Danica met his eyes in the mirror, and Grady took another mental snapshot of the gorgeous features that reflected back at him. The tides of his personal life were changing, Danica having washed in and out of his days for the past few weeks until this moment where they were both in the same place, focused on the same scene: each other.

He was racking up quite an impressive collection of beautiful mental snapshots from their day.

SEVENTEEN

Grady stood in front of the framed art he'd placed on the floor.

"Two paintings?" Iris put her hands on her hips, looking from Grady to his purchases.

He stood back to gauge their size. "They look about right."

He was all but ignoring Iris, and she raised her voice in protest to that. "But two?"

"They're matching ones. Sort of." He explained the booth from which he bought them at the weekend festival. "The artist showing them in San Antonio was from La Grange. She had some really impressive pieces, but these I liked the best."

Iris made a snide comment under her breath about wasting money on something that passes for art.

"This is art." If another person didn't see the beauty of colors and shapes come alive in three-D from a two-D canvas, he didn't want to bother to explain what that person was missing. Iris included. His eyes enjoyed the finished product. Now, every time he passed the pieces, he could also think about his wonderful Saturday in San Antonio with Danica. "Besides, I thought you'd be happy with some distraction on the walls for our patients, a way to prevent any more head-on column collisions."

Iris pushed her hip out, settling into a more confrontational pose. "We've only had one collision, and I'm sure you remember that."

Of course, he remembered. That was his first introduction to Danica, and he would have never guessed that encounter would be a foundation for a budding relationship. Still, Iris didn't know that Grady spent the best part of his weekend with her.

"What are you grinning about?" Iris now turned her attention away from the paintings and to Grady. "Don't tell me you're forgetting what could happen if someone like her tries to come back and sue us for negligence."

"We weren't negligent." This was the first time he and Iris were sharing the words, however, and any possibility that would rock the future of Spectacle Optique needed to be taken seriously. But he also knew he wasn't at fault. "It's not like we waxed the floors with vegetable oil or something ridiculous. These are just walls." He patted the brick column with his palm in the area where he planned to hang one of the paintings.

"Then why do you feel the need to cover them?" Iris interrogated.

Though it was a simple question, it rubbed him the wrong way. He told Iris so.

"I'm just wanting you to be careful." She backed down from her previous tone, softening her rigid stance as she did. "If you want to bring attention to the walls, it just seems like an acknowledgement that there was something not previously done that could have prevented her from smacking into it with a face plant."

Grady noted that Iris didn't say Danica's name, so he did. "Miss Lara is fine. We don't have to worry about any retribution from her."

"How can you be sure?"

"Because I saw her." He swallowed a gulp and then clarified. "I mean, I see her." They were simple words, but as soon as they escaped Grady's mouth, he wanted to take them back. He wasn't in a habit of sharing his personal life—even though there was very little to share—with anyone he employed, let alone Iris. He needed to be especially cautious with her to draw lines between their professional and private spheres.

Iris cast down her gaze. "You see her?"

Grady knew what Iris was hearing, and though he was a man in his thirties who could have a relationship of any kind with any individual he wanted, he flashed in that moment to being a teenager, standing before a girl who had a crush on him as he tried to communicate that he didn't share the same feelings. Did it ever get easier, this navigating the road of relationships? This encounter didn't make him believe so. He still wanted to be gentle toward Iris and in some way cradle this conversation with her, rocking toward a soft landing so their professional existence wouldn't crack.

Ill-prepared and not even knowing if Danica would confess to seeing Grady in a traditional relationship sense, he nonetheless admitted his view of the two of them. "Yes, I see her. She helped me pick these out."

Iris looked to the paintings with a face of disgust. "Oh."

Grady wasn't going to prolong the agony of more answers that Iris really didn't want to hear. He swerved back to his reasons for bringing the paintings inside in the first place. "It looks like these will work. Heath can help me hang them at the end of the day. I'll store them in the break room for now."

Iris spoke a single-syllable response of "great" with sarcasm that communicated the opposite.

Grady leaned down to retrieve the first painting.

"Is it serious?" Iris asked.

His relationship status with Danica was undefined between them. They kissed several times on Saturday, each more open and exploratory than the one before it. Their day was a give and take of shared time, shared laughter, and shared experiences with each other that, even now, reeled through Grady's memory in a mental album of portraits that was far greater than anything he could have anticipated. His romantic relationships of the past had always seemed planned. There was a calculated effort that made the process prescriptive, almost clinical. He ran his daily life like that, and not until this experience with Danica, did he realize that was the exact opposite of how a relationship needed to work for him.

Instead of planned, he needed spontaneous. Instead of effort, he needed something effortless. Instead of questioning if the next step was in line with some textbook progression of how others thought a relationship needed to go, he needed something that unfolded naturally.

And he had that.

"I'm seeing Danica Lara. And it's going well. I'm happy." That was the truth of it.

But Iris becoming a casualty of his admission wasn't a part of the plan.

Wetness dotted the corner of her eyes, and she squinted them in reaction as if they stung. "I hope that a lawsuit from her doesn't ruin your happiness." She turned on her heel, practically stomping away from Grady down the small hallway and into a workday that was going to be a long start to both their weeks.

~*~

Danica picked up her cell phone late Tuesday evening to an admonishment. "You have been avoiding me."

"Hello to you too." Danica knew Paige's voice, even when she tried to drop it an octave.

But her friend wasn't done with her verbal reprimand. "All weekend."

"I was gone Saturday."

"Precisely."

"And Sunday I didn't want to bother you when you were with your family—"

"Since when?" Paige had a way of ratcheting her voice that must have come from years of practice in motherhood. She knew how to use it toward Danica in such a way that weaseling out of conversation was pointless, yet she tried anyway.

Saturday was monopolized by Grady, and Sunday was her day of recovery from such an unexpectedly blissful time with him. Then Monday was the Labor Day holiday. She was in a swoony haze all day that she didn't want to break the spell with leaving the house or talking with anyone. Avoiding the risk, however, of sounding like a damsel in distress, she played coy with her friend. "I was busy."

And, typical for Paige, she read between the lines. "Busy?"

Even without seeing her face, Danica knew it was etched in skepticism. "That's right."

"Not buying it. Let's try again."

Danica huffed. "Really?"

"Don't try to hide anything from me. You were out. And I want details."

Danica switched ears, but she was still hearing Paige correctly. "On my Saturday?"

"Yes, on your Saturday." Her syllables were all sass. "Dish."

"And why is my personal life suddenly so interesting to you?"

"Because it involves Dr. McHottie."

There was that nickname again. Would she ever get Paige to shake it?

"Look, I'm a married woman who just put my son to bed. I have two loads of laundry keeping me company before I phone it in for the night. I need to live vicariously through someone."

"But Everett adores you." Surely, Paige's new

marriage wasn't souring.

"I never said he didn't. That man is a prince. One currently disguised as a chore boy in the kitchen because, last I saw, he was working on his dishpan hands and, I think, even packing Nathan's preschool snack for tomorrow." It sounded very routine, but also very sweet. "I'm not complaining in the least, but I'm also not the one having an out-of-town rendezvous—"

"Whoa!" She stopped her friend cold. "That word is a little brusque."

"Is it?" Now Paige was the one playing coy. "How would I know?"

Danica saw where this was going. "Fine."

"Just spill it."

And Danica did. All of it.

She started with the coffee stop Grady made on their way to San Antonio Saturday where they ordered the most amazing caramel lattes Danica had ever tasted.

"Mmmm," Paige voiced her appreciation as not only a fellow coffee lover but also, she presumed, as someone who saw value in a small gesture like that.

Danica gave a few navigational details of their arrival in downtown and then described how they jumped right into the thick of things.

"As you should." Paige knew the setup of the arts and crafts show. "Lots to see."

"Exactly." She told her friend about a few of the vendors. Described a handful of the most interesting ones. Apprised the ratio of jewelry to art.

"Now get to the good stuff." Her friend hurried

her along to more private details.

Danica knew the level of dishing Paige wanted to hear, but the truth was "It was all good."

"I bet it was." She returned the words as if they had been tapped with a ping-pong paddle through the phone call.

"Do you want to hear about this or not?" Though, at this point, Danica wasn't even sure she wanted to share details that had been such a source of private pleasure.

"That's why I called," she insisted. Paige held silence on the line, giving Danica the platform to speak. "And I won't interrupt."

"You have."

"Try me again."

And how long would that last? But Danica reasoned that any chance to think about Grady, even in sharing those thoughts, was time well spent. So, she took a deep breath and launched into the most romantic of details that were best-friend worthy.

Easy conversation, shared laughter, successful shopping, and tender kisses pretty much characterized the day. Danica highlighted the broad strokes of their trip to help Paige see them, but she kept the more intimate details—that look she knew from Grady's eyes but couldn't quite put into words as well as the sensational smoothness of his kisses—to herself.

A long pause on Paige's end followed by a dreamy sigh capped her reaction. "You, my dear, are in deep."

"I don't think I'd call it that."

"Call it what you want," she breezed. "But I'm

happy for you."

Danica felt her friend's support in spite of their physical distance at the moment. "Thanks. I'm happy too." Even though Danica wasn't sure about an exact label, this was a relationship with Grady. And she didn't need to define it any more than that.

She basked in the glow of talking about Grady, feeling every bit as optimistic about some sort of future with him as she had on Saturday. He stirred happiness inside of her, using what she was old enough to recognize as a no-games approach to being a couple. They didn't need to announce partnerdom on some stage, plaster it across social media, or even call it dating aloud. Their time together cemented a connection.

Now, what she could do was admit to Paige, "It just feels right." It's not like Danica was active in a hunt for a relationship, and her rustiness, perhaps, had turned into a strength here. She wasn't rushed, and she had no expectations. But that simply made the discovery of Grady sweeter. He was a right fit for her. "Kind of like a market match," she added, unable to avoid a real estate reference. She waited for Paige to respond, but instead, she had to prompt her into a reply when her friend stayed silent. "Paige?"

"I'm still here." But something about her voice wasn't right. She struck a melancholy chord.

"Paige?" Danica prompted again, sensing the shift. "What's wrong?"

She heard a deep inhale through the line as if Paige were gathering enough air to repeat the syllables in one of Danica's last words. "Market. That made me think about something."

"What?"

"Barry." She plunked her ex-husband's name into the conversation and swerved their conversation into a concern about him. "Has he said anything to you?"

"About what?" Certainly, what she did with Grady was of no consequence to Barry.

"The development at Cinnamon Ridge. You don't have to tell me—"

"I'll tell you whatever you want to hear," she assured. She was not going to keep a secret from her friend. Propagating the project had taken place without the knowledge of Paige, and it was something Danica deeply regretted. She never intended to hurt her by agreeing to a partnership with Barry to develop the subdivision. Indirectly, however, she had hurt Paige when she found out on her own. While Danica couldn't take that back, she could work hard to assure her friend of straightforward, legal dealings. All her cards were on the table, and she wasn't going to hide anything.

Paige cleared her throat. "Can you tell me if it's profitable yet?"

That was an easy question to answer, though a disappointing one. "No. The infrastructure investment has been more expensive than we thought. And we haven't sold any lots. That scale will tip, but it hasn't yet."

"I see." Paige took her time before she articulated a second question. "Are you OK financially?"

"I will be." Saying the words aloud made her believe them. "But waiting is the hard part."

"It always is," Paige conceded.

With her friend, Danica could be completely honest. "I just thought this would be easier than it is. I don't know if that was my naïveté or just wishful thinking."

"You can be wishful. There's nothing wrong with that."

"Maybe." Danica exhaled deeply. "But it's a little exhausting at times."

"Think of it as a gentle reminder of adulthood." Paige offered the advice in her own careful way. Greed wasn't in her DNA, and neither was judgment. Still, she had friendship at the forefront of every pep talk she gave Danica. "Stay positive. Good things will come."

That was easy for Paige to say. Speaking in fortune cookie optimism was a fine approach, but it was hard to sustain in the throes of real estate uncertainty.

EIGHTEEN

How could women live without their intuition?

Danica had listened to her inner voice countless times over the years. Friends and female coworkers with whom she spoke had done the same. Whether it was a byproduct of nature or nurture, the fact was that women listened to their guts.

So what was a woman to do when her gut wasn't talking?

Danica tapped the side of her waist as if doing so would awaken a dormant voice that lay deep inside of her. The peculiar part of all of this was that her intuition was telling her to open herself to Grady. And to open herself to mentoring Owen. She had done both those things, and the short-term results of those, at least, were positive. Her heart was happy in the company of Grady, and her mind was beginning to stretch Owen's in small ways that she hoped were making a big difference for him with literacy. Yet on matters of Barry, her inner voice was silent.

She heeded Paige's words after their Tuesday phone call, avowing to stay positive. Yet she wasn't going to let doubt cloud her judgment. She decided to take a second look over bills and contracts that bore both Danica and Barry's names as co-developers.

When Paige asked about profitability, she wasn't out of line. It was a fair question to ask friend to friend, especially with their likeness in day jobs.

The bottom line wasn't anywhere in the black for her, and she had thought Barry was equally in the red.

But she discovered a surprise about that.

As she started charting, calculating, and crunching the numbers in half, she realized something wasn't right.

And it was completely her fault that she was doing all of this on her lunch break in the appraisal district break room. She wanted—needed—to talk to Barry about this, but reaching out to make a call was too dangerous. Cameron's reprimand still loomed, and she would suck her thumb in the office before she'd make a move that would jeopardize her job.

Again.

Still, it took every ounce of restraint for Danica to calmly return to her desk after her lunchtime discovery and not focus on why she had a bill for an asphalt company that included a line-item for materials that had previously been billed separately. Or why she had yet to see a bill at all from the general contractor with whom she spoke about the water lines several weeks ago. She had saved the pecan grove she wanted, though two smaller trees had to be removed from the main road's right-of-way. Shouldn't the local company who the contractor hired to do that have sent the invoice for their labor by now?

Danica lashed herself with a mental reprimand. How did she let paperwork like this slide? What else was falling through the cracks? Was Barry's sloppiness in handling this project affecting their bottom line? She needed to be more involved, and she needed to stay on top of this if she was going to net anywhere close to the profits she anticipated when she said yes to this scheme that she was now regretting.

As Danica leaned over the copy machine to make sets for an upcoming in-house file audit, Cameron approached behind her. "Are those for my review?"

"Yes." Danica grabbed a small stack that had already collated and stapled. "Do you want to begin with these?"

"Sure." She accepted the files into her arms. "A head start is always good."

"Right." Danica offered a tight-lipped smile and spoke over the noise of the machine. "Do you want me to put the rest on your desk when I'm done?"

"That would be fine."

Danica still walked on eggshells around this woman. "Yes, ma'am. I'll do that."

"I'll also need some deed comparisons pulled. Can you get those to me by the end of the day?"

"Absolutely." This was the part of her job that overlapped with Paige's world at the Land & Title Office, and any excuse to call her or reach out with a question would add a little more sanity to an otherwise doldrum day. "Do you have a list of properties?"

"I'll e-mail it." Cameron clarified the property types. "Residential lots, mostly. Undeveloped. But we're trying to get a better handle on appraised values with this real estate surge."

Danica nodded, knowing Cinnamon Ridge was sandwiched right in the thick of it with a few others. If Cameron was referring to Danica's project, it was in such a slight way that Danica chose not to dwell on it. Yet researching comparable values for sites similar to what Barry and she were doing would be a great way to see if their proposed ideas for asking prices were in line with current market values now or if they needed to raise or lower what they originally anticipated as asking prices for each lot.

Raise, raise, raise. Danica chanted a mental mantra as a wish more than anything. There didn't seem to be an opportunity to increase her full-time salary anytime soon, and certainly, the black mark in her personnel file from that reprimand wouldn't help if it did.

Money wasn't everything, but this project was a one-time opportunity to boost her finances. She needed to see Cinnamon Ridge to fruition, and she needed to do it the right way. "I'll get started on that list."

Cameron nodded her thanks and headed back to her desk with an armful of paperwork, leaving Danica with a mindset of staying the course with Barry. Through was the only way forward at this point. Her intuition at least told her that much.

~*~

A still lingering breeze mid Friday morning was a sign that the season of autumn wasn't far around the corner. The kids were settling into back-to-school mode, and according to what Grady saw with Mrs.

Livingston leading the mentoring pack, they were doing well.

The third graders came up to him one by one with a quick and happy report of their reading.

"I'm following your book prescription, Dr. Urban," one beamed.

"Twenty minutes a day." Another child pumped a series of high fives in the air to signify the total.

"My mom won't let me play video games until after I read," said another, though there seemed to be no love lost in the way the boy spoke the words. Perhaps this was just a new routine, and he wasn't seeing it as a negative one.

Hearing that the children were reading was as exciting for Grady as it was for Mrs. Livingston. "You have no idea the difference this makes." She put a hand on Grady's shoulder. "Those book prescriptions were a great idea."

"I'll continue to check in with them if that's what it takes."

Mrs. Livingston probably would have hugged Grady if there weren't so much other activity at the moment with DEAR time starting. "You are a gem, Dr. Urban. An absolute sparkler." She squeezed his shoulder as she said a word Grady used for Danica's eyes. Just hearing it gave him a reason to think of her, which warmed him.

But he didn't have long to do so before his attention was elsewhere.

Mrs. Livingston lowered her hand from Grady as quickly as she had placed it before she turned to the center of the room and made an attention-grabbing clap. "Children, let's take our seats."

Alexis approached Grady with a small piece of paper outstretched. "What's this?" He took the crumpled book prescription from her and turned it over to see a series of numbers and times. Each line item had an abbreviation for a day of the week, and the number twenty was circled at the end of the pencil calculations. "Have you been reading every day?"

Alexis nodded a shy smile before she whispered as if trusting him with a playground secret. "Sometimes more than twenty."

"Good for you." Grady was proud of all the kids, but Alexis's dedication as his mentee held a special place in his heart. "Books are great friends to spend time with, wouldn't you say?"

She bit her lip, showing the toothless spot in her upper row of teeth as she sat down.

"Let's see your progress." He slid today's book selection to her, and she began reading with more confidence than Grady had seen in the previous weeks.

All around them, there were happy pairings as children took leads in reading, shared their improvements, and shone with excitement for their new skills. Although he appreciated Mrs. Livingston's saying so, it wasn't really the book prescriptions that had the greatest impact. It was the collective, community approach. Here were people who cared about progress with students, who were willing to give generously of their time to help students be more successful. Magic seemed to happen within the walls of this classroom space, and Grady was grateful that he'd gotten to be a part of it.

Some magic, too, was finally starting to happen between Danica and Owen.

Grady knew that Danica had, with Mrs. Livingston's support, contacted the school counselor about Owen's summer injury. In cooperation with the school nurse and the school's speech pathologist, they all communicated this week with Owen's teacher to have him work on some critical thinking and problem-solving skills that would, little by little, help him rebuild his cognition. Danica had kept Grady informed as they chatted a couple of times during the week, and today when he looked over to them, Owen seemed to have a focus and level of interest that had previously been lacking.

Danica managed a thumbs-up sign to Grady when she caught him looking her way a second time, so he took that as the best sign of all.

The end of the DEAR time came too soon for Grady's taste.

And apparently for Alexis. "It's over already?" She pouted in the cutest, most mollifying way possible.

"Children," Mrs. Livingston called their attention again. "We are going to put away our books five minutes early today so that we can all get our artwork."

Grady still chuckled to himself at the way this teacher spoke in the collective voice with the children, as if she were in the exact boat with them.

And seeing the joy Mrs. Livingston had for her job,

it wasn't surprising to Grady that she did speak that way.

"Come, children." She motioned for them to gather round her like little lambs, and she had each of them take turns to choose their artwork from a large paper portfolio. Then they lined up across the front of the room holding their artwork in front of them for all the mentors to see. "Presenting, the Seguin Elementary School's vision of Back to School!" She flourished with her hand as the company of mentors broke into applause from their seats in the classroom.

Danica turned to Grady and mouthed "impressive." He concurred. Bright slashes of color, sharp outlines, and cartoonish interpretations of books, school buses, backpacks, smiling stick figures, and all manner of sun, clouds, hearts, and flowers decorated the children's artwork. Each child beamed from behind his or her picture, and Grady was crowning this project another successful one, even without them yet being hung in Spectacle Optique's display window.

But once he returned to the office with the stack of artwork, it didn't take long for Samantha to do that. By day's end, the office's front window was transformed into a festive color explosion. Samantha strung a line from one side of the glass to the other and hung each child's picture with clothespins. She chose a couple to set against cardboard as makeshift easels next to the construction paper-covered boxes she stacked like giant building blocks. Ever an eye for optometry design, she kept a few select frames as well as one small promotional flyer for a vendor reminding passersby of a discount that they could get on a certain brand of contact lenses. Finally, she made a simple sign to display in the center of the scene that announced the artwork and the name of the children's school as well as a couple of lines about DEAR time.

"This turned out so well." Grady stood along with Iris and Heath, who all took a quick break to see the fruits of Samantha's labor. "Bravo!"

"Bravo to you," Samantha returned. "It was all your idea."

"I'm just glad it came together like this." Grady really couldn't believe it.

"Yes, congratulations, Dr. Urban." Iris's voice was all saccharine. She capped her comment with a surprise lean toward Grady, unnerving him with a sideways hug. If Samantha or Heath noticed the awkwardness, neither said anything.

Grady simply cleared his throat and shifted his stance to keep his posture as Iris regrouped after his lack of physical reciprocation. He wasn't interested in entertaining a game with Iris or playing on her emotions, knowing they were fragile. Besides, the only woman he really cared to hug was in the appraisal district building, and he hoped she was having a similarly happy afternoon.

~*~

After a trying day at the office, Danica was ready to head home.

Her only consolation was that Barry had not

contacted her by phone during work hours, and he'd refrained from stepping into the office.

Whereas she had to teach Barry about boundaries, Grady was the opposite. He didn't contact her during the day. Yet two minutes after five o'clock when Grady knew Danica was officially off the clock, he pinged her cell phone with a text that urged her to come by the office. He had something to show her.

It didn't take much for her to swing that direction instead of heading home, as any opportunity to see Grady was one she took. Her evenings were completely flexible anyway, so if they decided on an impromptu dinner, that was fine by her.

But dinner wasn't on Grady's radar, at least not when Danica arrived at the optometry office. From the sidewalk, she was able to see the surprise. The children's artwork hung in a vibrant display that filled her with instantaneous happiness. It was hard not to smile at the carefully crafted pictures that shone with elementary school pride.

Grady waved at her from inside the shop, and she raised her hands to clap her approval for this job well done. He took a mock bow before urging her again, this time opening the door for her. After he did so, he leaned in to greet Danica with a kiss on the cheek. "Hi there."

She was becoming fond of his kisses, yet this was a little too light for the kind of day Danica had. She needed a dose of affection a little stronger.

A quick glance revealed they were alone, as far as her eyes could tell, and she positioned herself more fully in front of Grady, sensually peering up at him. "Hi there to you." She lifted onto slight tiptoes and met his lips with her own.

After that sweet yet satisfying move that communicated how much she had missed him, she pulled back to look at him. His eyes shone as he raised his lids, his glasses framing his gorgeous gaze as if with picture frames. "You know I'm getting used to kissing with glasses." She bit her lower lip in fun.

"I hope that doesn't mean you're just randomly kissing guys with glasses," he teased.

She reached to his shoulder, squeezing against it as she commented on his humor. "You don't have anything to worry about there." She leaned in close, whispering, "Besides, I only have eyes for my optometrist."

"Clever." He winked, another move of his that made her melt on the inside.

Danica's built-up stress of the day, which she'd kept inside, now morphed into something warm, wonderful...and Urban. She locked her gaze with this doctor, a superhero beneath the white coat whom she was pleased to have discovered. Maybe she didn't always handle stress at her job in the best way or maybe she didn't always make the right decisions when it came to land development, but when it came to this matter of the heart, Danica felt like her intuition was guiding her in all the right places. She pointed with her thumb over her shoulder to the display window. "That is a beautiful surprise."

"It turned out so well, didn't it?" He kept his

hands on each side of her, as if warming her and not wanting to let her go. "But that's not the surprise I called about."

"It's not?" Danica puzzled.

"There's something else I want you to see," Grady baited.

"Oh? Now what would that be?"

Grady took her by the hand. "Follow me." He led her around the corner to the patient hallway where he unveiled his reason with a "Ta da!"

On one wall was the canvas they purchased second from the San Antonio show, and on the column that she knew more intimately from meeting it with her forehead was the canvas that caught both their eyes and led to their first kiss. "You didn't waste any time getting these hung."

"I was eager to look at them." Grady beamed with child-like enthusiasm. "So, what do you think?"

But before Danica had time to answer, a woman interrupted. "Sorry, I didn't know you still had a patient here." Iris stepped into view, but she wasn't wearing her clinical overcoat. A low-cut top and tight skirt made her look a little more party-ready than professional.

Danica stepped into view from around Grady's side and gave a wave. "Not a patient. Or not today."

"Oh." Iris gave a territorial "hi."

Grady, ever the broker to a surprise situation, told Iris that he invited her to see the paintings. "And I was just asking her what she thought."

Iris crossed her arms over her chest, pushing her

cleavage up a notch. There was nothing subtle about this woman. "So, what do you think?"

Danica wasn't sure if she was just asking about the art.

To test, Danica gave an ambiguous answer. "I think these are just perfect." She looked from one canvas to another, but she squeezed Grady's hand, willing him not to let go.

"That's what I think." Iris took a step toward the one that hung against the column. "It should help people see this wall a little better." She patted against the bricks. "After all, we don't want anyone to have another accident like you had." She forced an awkward chuckle. "That would give somebody reason to sue this place, and no one needs that."

Danica wasn't sure if those words were a warning—or a jab. Was a potential lawsuit on this new business's radar? Could it have been on Grady's? Surely, the potential that she might make such a move toward Spectacle Optique wasn't part of his reason for getting her close. But even as the questions raced through her mind, her gut was turning in confusion. She dropped her hand from Grady's, surprised by her own quick action.

Iris uncrossed her arms and raised one in a flirty-fingered wave. "Well, I'm off then." She pivoted with cheerleader-like perk to disappear as quickly as she had appeared, leaving Danica in a wake of confusion with a seed of doubt planted.

Had Grady gotten close to her only to prevent a lawsuit? Was he worried about retribution for an injury Danica had already forgotten? Clearly the office hadn't. Otherwise, Iris wouldn't have mentioned it. She turned to Grady for answers. "What was that about?"

Grady brought a hand to his forehead, rubbing his temple. "I really don't know."

Danica's intuition wasn't always right, but even now, it pulled at her to listen. And it was telling her Grady really did know.

Maybe this relationship—or whatever they were or weren't calling it—was more of a distraction to save his business than anything real. And that was enough to cause Danica to pivot just as sharply as Iris and turn away from Grady, retracing her steps to head out of the building and guard her heart before he could do any damage to something she thought was a genuine relationship.

"Wait!" Grady called after her, but it was too late. This was just like her mistakes with the development project. She entered in with good intentions, thought the other person in the mix was being transparent, only to discover a secret agenda. Danica already had enough complications with Barry, and she didn't need any with Grady. A sharp sense of betrayal made her flee. As she left the office, she raised her guard and didn't even look back.

She was done listening to Grady, and she was done continuing anything with him. She had heard and seen enough.

NINETEEN

Eight years of pre-med classes and optometry school had fortified Grady with a wide array of knowledge, enough that he felt motivated to open his own office. But comfort wasn't what he lacked. What was missing from him in the role of leader in the office was confidence. And comfort and feeling confidence were two different things.

But that stopped now.

Watching Danica turn away from him and refuse to even hear him out was a blow that, as hard as it was to acknowledge, was a direct result of his lack of intervention, even more his lack of placating Iris's intrusion in his personal life in the first place. He thought he had drawn a pretty clear line after Samantha's breakup that the office could be personable but would stay professional. Getting involved in intimate details of another's personal life was not to be commonplace.

As he was left standing alone, though, he second-guessed everything.

His ability to communicate with his employees.

His balancing of professional life with a private life.

His ability to even hold a relationship with

another female.

He was still indebted with student loans for years of optometry school, but now Grady wished he had a secondary degree in interpersonal communication, for none of his higher education had prepared him for this.

Alone for the first time since this morning, he looked around from wall to ceiling to floor, all part of what he had built. He didn't use his hands, but it was his vision, his expertise, and his commitment which conceived this place and which had managed to get it off the ground.

But no man was an island.

Without his employees, he couldn't keep this place going. Samantha was a workhorse and completely invaluable. So, too, was Heath, who did more on the retail side than he originally conceived was needed.

And then there was Iris.

An optometrist needed a technician. True, he could get by in some instances without one, but ultimately it was an assistant who performed half of the work that allowed Grady to focus on the use of his skills. Iris asked questions about a patient's medical history, started the exam process, and even ran some procedures and therapies. She knew the equipment. She was organized with their inventory, and she was efficient when it came to patient rotation. He needed that assistance just like he needed the assistance that each of his employees brought to the table.

But no office needed personal sabotage.

He wasn't running a high school newspaper staff. Gossip, personal agendas, or a crush needed to stop.

And he needed to be the one to put a stop to it. Before he could handle Danica, he needed to handle Iris.

Grady ran after her, catching her as she grabbed her lunch bag from the break room and almost headed out the building. "What was that about?"

She swung the door of the refrigerator closed and looked with doe eyes, as if she'd just been caught drinking from a milk carton. "What do you mean?"

"Stop." He mustered every bit of professional confidence he had. "Don't do this. Not to yourself, not to me."

"Did Danica leave?"

"That was your intent, wasn't it?"

Iris shrugged. "I'm not one to run off patients."

"You did." Grady squared his shoulders. "And you won't do it again." He didn't want to play bad cop, but asserting some authority was needed in this situation. "This is a business, and I value my employees. But business is not personal, not when it comes to relationships. I have no interest in blurring those lines, ever. No routines, no special cases." It was all Grady could do not to use her name and make this strictly about her, though it was.

Iris hugged her lunch bag to her chest. "I understand."

"Don't do this to yourself," Grady counseled, his voice softening. "I'm trying to give everyone a career here, and I want this to be a cooperative work environment, not a stressful one. We come to work, we interact, but there are no relationships. I develop that outside of the office." The tug to now run toward

Danica was strong, but he needed to finish this so that he could make things right. "And if you want a relationship, I suggest you find someone outside of the office with whom to develop it too."

Iris shifted her lunch bag, placing it next to her as she grabbed the handle. Her face drained of all the previous theatrics. "I'm sorry."

Grady didn't want to give her a false impression with any buildup for compliments, but he did offer, "Explore the area because good people are everywhere. I found one when I wasn't even looking." His attention pulled again toward Danica. "And now I need to see if she's still willing to give something with me a shot."

Iris apologized again, adding, "No more blurred lines. I'll leave you to it." She stepped toward Grady, angling her shoulder to ease past him before sliding back into work routine language with a "see you tomorrow" farewell.

Grady stood alone only long enough to realize alone wasn't what he wanted to be. So he cut the lights, locked the door behind Iris, and grabbed his phone to give Danica a call.

~*~

Danica drove to what was once empty acreage. Years ago, the land was decisively in the rural space of Guadalupe County. With decades of growth, sprawl along the outskirts of Seguin grew wider, making the land inch more toward improvements with each passing year. By the time it was available for purchase, the space was ripe for development.

Barry Van Soyt had seen this, his home inspection eye turning toward greater profit with the land's possibility. He first approached Danica at the appraisal district office when he caught wind of a rumored sale, heading it off at the pass before the owner could list it. Barry had gotten Danica's assistance with determining fair market value, and even her eyes saw what Barry's did when they crunched the numbers.

Land development wasn't a project either had planned to undertake, but the possibility was before them. They drew a basic contract between them, co-signed a bank note, and were both listed on the new deed. Twenty lots were to be sold, and after the investment they made in infrastructure with attractive signage at the entrance, buried utilities, cul-de-sac streets, and proper curbing, they could turn a heavy profit.

As Danica parked her vehicle along the street and gazed across the development in progress, she could envision it all. So much was taking shape, and even with hiccups in their partnership, she still believed in this project. True, she was seeking a return on her investment, but she also believed in the power of being able to help people afford a place of their own. By dividing this acreage, she was doing that for nearly two dozen families. She hoped they would fall in love with Seguin as she had, becoming life-long residents who would ultimately share in their own investments of the community, whether that was through building families, starting businesses, or volunteering in the area.

Volunteering. Danica guffawed how her thoughts turned back to something she shared with Grady. He was perhaps the poster child, now that she considered it, of the type of buyer she hoped to attract. Professional, caring, committed. Growth for the sake of growth wasn't what she sought. She wanted individuals like him who would make their community a better place.

Danica opened the door of her car, stood atop the asphalt, and let a breeze whirl her hair as the sun kissed the ends. She closed her eyes, setting her face to the glow from the horizon line, barely visible through the grove of trees she'd managed to save. She rested her arms on the opened door and nestled her chin against them to enjoy the view of day's end.

Someday, residents would be enjoying this view. New couples, established partners, families, and maybe one day the children of their children would see what Danica was seeing. The glory of a day's end igniting the sky in majestic colors created a canvas of beauty that filled Danica with satisfaction even during an otherwise unsatisfying day.

The only interruption to the placid view was a buzz from her cell phone. She glanced to the screen from the upturned device on her passenger's seat, and when she saw the name, she decided to answer.

She leaned in to grab the phone before cradling it to her ear as she resumed her stance to watch the sun sink lower and lower. "I'm outside." It seemed to be a fitting greeting for the caller.

"Should that surprise me?" He returned an unorthodox reply.

"It may if you knew where I was standing." Rays of light continued to radiate in pleasing patterns of too many colors to count. "Want to take a guess?"

"How many do I get?"

"I should only give you one."

"That's making it easy on me," he perked. "I'm glad you're there because I've got good news."

"Barry," she started, knowing he only generally called with bad news, "if this is some joke—"

"It's not a joke."

It was hard to believe Barry Van Soyt.

"I promise. Hear me out."

"Fine." She shook back her hair, toying with the breeze as much as it toyed with her. "Shoot."

"I should probably do this in person, actually. Now that I think about it, maybe if you're standing there and I could—"

"Barry." Danica snapped him back into focus with her voice. Typical, the way he always seemed to give the run-around. He wasn't a malicious person by nature. When it came to social cues and expectations, Barry seemed to be one of those people who fell short. "Just get on with it."

Barry stuttered through another "oh, OK" before finding his rhythm enough to reveal the reason for his call.

And it was a doozy.

"We made our first sale. Times two."

Danica had to let the double-whammy of investment news sink in. "Two lots?"

"Yes. Sold."

"To whom? When?" There was so much she wanted to ask, but short questions seemed to be all she could form at the moment.

"Today."

"Done deal?"

"It will be."

Danica ran a hand down the length of her hair, stroking away surprise and stress. This is what she had been waiting for—what they both had been waiting for—in taking on the investment in the first place. Sales were the ultimate goal, and they had both thought they would have to work a little harder to get the first one.

Maybe Barry had.

For all Danica knew, he was hustling behind the scenes. He was peculiar, the way he could annoy so easily yet shock so unexpectedly. This time, at least, the shock was a good thing.

"Take me through everything. I want to know."

Barry told her more details about the couple who purchased two lots. One, he explained, was going to be used for building their own home, a four-bedroom two story. They wanted the other lot as a temporary buffer from neighbors, but they might resell it somewhere down the road.

"That's fine." Danica interjected. "We had already talked about that." The possibility was one she and Barry both decided was acceptable, as long as the buyer was willing to fork over the same asking price.

"And they did, right?" Danica held her breath; if there was going to be any bad news delivered with the good, this would be it.

"We got our full asking price. No negotiation." At those words, relief spread through Danica. "And I've already gone to Paige at the Land & Title Office. The ball's rolling."

Two lots, sold.

Danica drew the signs in her mind's eye and stared at the land before her, imagining how staking two such signs would look.

And feel.

Future homes were taking shape thanks to the work she and Barry had already done for Cinnamon Ridge. What was once just an idea was coming into full fruition.

"Incredible." That's all Danica could breathe to express her happiness.

"I know," Barry echoed. There was a realization in his voice at how big of a step this was, how much this meant. For him, no doubt, it was as validating as it was to Danica. But Barry also had financial responsibilities that extended to Nathan. His son's future depended on this project as much as anyone's.

Given all the involvement and all the hiccups of their communication, Danica was glad to be out of the loop with Barry in this particular instance. She still had some questions about the irregularity of paperwork she found, and she told Barry she wanted to sit with him to go over everything. He agreed, but even those bills were small amounts compared to the money they were going to get now. The surprise had been worth it. She tried to force mental math into her racing thoughts. "That's an incredible return already."

"I know. I think it would be smart to take this money and put some of it toward that promotional campaign we talked about. We need the outreach in marketing to San Antonio publications, and then we can use those listing services online."

"I agree." Danica did, and she expected that marketing would have to be done before any sale. Now, with two of the twenty lots already taken, they could use those sold percentages in their literature and drum up some immediacy for buyers to act fast before other lots went as well.

"Do you still have that list we collected?"

"I'm on it." Marketing was something Danica could do. "I'll look over it this evening and e-mail it to you."

They discussed a few more particulars before Barry told her he'd be in touch when the paperwork was ready to sign. He parted with a "we did it" congratulations.

"I'm so happy about this." Danica returned the sentiment. Sales were the goal, and having this momentum so early was a positive sign.

Holding the phone at her side, Danica felt weight melt from her shoulders. Had Cinnamon Ridge really taken so much mental and physical energy?

Yes.

She took the opportunity to let the project pressures slide away as she savored a newfound self-confidence that came from pride in what she had undertaken. She looked at the spot that was once just flat land, her new turquoise glasses taking in a different view than weeks before. Her prescription magnified the improvements that she had a hand in making to this area. She had always liked this land, and now she appreciated the loveliness of the tracts she and Barry had worked with the contractor to design. Already, a buyer had seen what they had seen and was willing to pay top dollar for it.

She was proud of her vision. Maybe before every tract was sold, she would think more seriously about staking one for herself. A spot at the end of the last cul-de-sac would be divine. That location wouldn't be a far drive from Paige's house or terribly far from the appraisal district's office either. Yet it would be an individual dwelling.

She was, after all, single.

Danica brought her hand to her blue topaz pendant, sliding it along the length of her necklace chain absently. Her thoughts turned to Grady, and she wondered how much of their connection and communication was built on a relationship anyway. More likely, it was built as a buffer against any possible lawsuit Danica might bring toward his burgeoning business. She knew how investments worked. Now, she could kick herself for not realizing the shallow foundation on which a relationship—and could she even call it that?—had been built. He was only trying to stave off legal action. That was disappointing to Danica on so many levels.

Danica wasn't the type of person Iris insinuated. That Grady didn't stand up for her or even realize so himself was as disheartening as anything.

But even those events weren't going to cast a negative shadow across Danica's good news.

She had a gorgeous late afternoon view on display before her, and her profitable real estate news was enough to keep her daydreaming for what remained of the day. It didn't make her completely forget her emotions just half an hour earlier, but it was a pleasant counteraction to them.

Nonetheless, leave it to technology to serve as a reminder of what she would have liked to forget. Danica was so wrapped up in her conversation with Barry and the afterglow of good news that she didn't realize she missed a call from Grady until she raised her phone. When she slid her thumb across the screen of her phone, she saw his name. Then, she checked for a message, but there wasn't one.

Just as well. Calling her had probably been a mistake.

TWENTY

Tonight was an insta-dinner night.

Cooking for one person was tough, and that was on a good night.

This was decidedly not one of those.

Grady was open to experimentation and was actually a decent cook who'd turned even better with a few recipes Samantha had floated his way. But cooking after a hard day's work was tough on weeknights unless he had a specific reason to do so, which meant he usually had something semi-homemade instead. He was skilled at bagel pizza making and a four-can stew he concocted. For something more refined, he rotated between gourmet grilled cheese and deli turkey meat with pesto sandwiches thrown into a Panini press. It was the one gadget in his kitchen that he actually used, foolproof and fail-proof.

Unlike his love life.

He didn't want to take any chances with dinner tonight, and a five-minute microwave meal was too convenient to resist. He punched the time on the panel of the microwave to start it and then leaned against the kitchen counter with the frozen dinner box. Taste of India, it read. The sodium count alone was enough to season all of Mumbai. Grady sighed, the distinctive tang of curry meeting his nostrils and teasing his hunger with the digital countdown on the display screen.

Grady hoped the added ginger, garlic, and chili seasoning of the dish would mask the bitter taste left in his mouth by the events of the day.

He had been so excited to show Danica the canvases along the hallway of Spectacle Optique, pleased with the way they looked after being hung. Several repeat patients commented on them, all favorable. Every time Grady passed them, he thought of Danica.

More.

And more.

And more.

After all, he passed by the artwork lots of times during the day.

The third graders' window display had turned out swimmingly as well, and Grady anticipated nothing but smiles from Danica as he showed off the new additions. Instead, she walked away in near tears. That devastation and the cold shoulder from a misunderstanding were his last images of her.

He wasn't even sure where to hang his frustration. He was so out of practice with the workings of a relationship. He was successful with patient exams, marching them in, assessing their needs, and giving them what he could. Why was it so different with a romance? His analytical mind turned through the steps he took—along with the steps he should have taken. Where had he gone wrong?

"Everywhere," he sighed. He'd stayed quiet when he should have spoken up, and he should never have let Danica walk away. Nor should he have ever put her in a position to do so, even if it was based on a misunderstanding. Iris had gone too far, but Grady felt he could have put a stop to her more explicitly than he did. Now, though, all he could do was turn over possibilities in his mind of what should have been done rather than what was done.

The timer on the microwave signaled the end of the cooking cycle, and he removed the insta-meal with a quick grab. He had to drop the flimsy container on the counter nearly as fast as he had picked it up, the pads of his fingers burning with heat.

Grady waved his right hand, which took the brunt of the temperature. "Not the first time today I've been burned." He eyed the steaming dish as he talked to it as if the spurting and bubbling of the sauce around the edges had initiated this edgy conversation.

Grady rubbed his hand on his jeans. "Talking to a microwave dinner, really? No more speaking aloud," he told himself, half humored and half mortified at the pathetic scene. The person with whom he really wanted to speak hadn't answered his call earlier, and he couldn't blame Danica for that. Clearly, when she walked away from him at the office, she had no intention of turning right back around. Still, that was the exact reaction Grady wanted.

Turn around.

Listen to an explanation.

Stay.

But Grady couldn't control Danica any more than he could control what was beneath the film of his previously frozen dinner. He peeled back the layer on the dish, releasing an intensified aroma of what had already begun to fill his small kitchen. Tonight was him and Vindaloo. Though if he had it his way, it would have been him and Danica.

~*~

Danica's tears drowned out her words.

"Slow down." Paige counseled Danica into trying again. "Start over."

Danica sniffled through her words, still not able to deliver something coherent. Her cell phone caught a few of the tears that had nowhere else to land.

Paige continued to coach Danica through a series of mantras that took the edge off. "Take a deep breath."

Danica tried.

"Now another."

Danica did.

"Take your time. I've got all night."

That was sweet of Paige to say, but Danica knew it wasn't true. "You've got a four-year-old who probably wants a bedtime story."

"Everett's got it covered. I've already said good night to Nathan." She assuaged Danica's reservations. "My friend needs me, and I'm here. So, what's going on?"

Danica continued with another deep breath, ready

to talk about the emotions that had swirled from anger to shock to happiness to frustration. Grady, Iris, Barry...she didn't know where to place her negative feelings, nor did she know how to separate the positive ones. She should have been so happy tonight with the Cinnamon Ridge news, but it was overshadowed by a pit of despair at losing Grady.

Losing. She realized this was the first time she was truly naming the event, even if it was only in her mind. And it all felt like her fault.

She wanted to unload everything on Paige, as much for her own sake as anything. "I don't even know where to start."

"Wherever you want."

Paige's listening ear was one quality of her friend she appreciated the most. And that was even with her ex-husband in the mix.

"Please," Paige breezed when Danica made mention of Barry. "Remember: with me, it's a no-judgment zone."

So Danica began.

She found her voice enough to articulate the jumble inside of her. Even so, it wasn't easy. "Why is everything so confusing sometimes?"

"Because we're human." Paige's solidarity shone. "We feel so many different things."

"You can say that again." As Danica continued, it wasn't long before she experienced release just by getting the words out to someone. Friendship was her therapy, and Paige was her personal counselor tonight.

Danica spoke with Paige about the lot sales.

Surely, Paige would be receiving paperwork soon at the Land & Title Office. But Danica was glad to be the first to tell Paige, who offered shared congratulations and enthusiastic comments. "I know you've worked hard for this. And it certainly hasn't been easy."

Understatement.

"But you did it."

True, Danica was a part of the process by virtue of her co-development role. Still, "I don't even know how to take credit. It's not like I found the buyers or showed them the property. Barry did all of that."

"Good." Paige didn't miss a beat. "Let him do that. He can be responsible for some sales, but ultimately it's the work that you have put in, too, over the long haul that makes it possible."

Logically, Danica knew that. "I guess I just thought I would feel different."

"How?" Paige joked, "Confetti and balloons falling from the sky?"

Danica didn't know.

Apparently, Paige sensed that. "What's really bothering you?"

The heart of it was Grady. That was, after all, where Danica felt the hole. Then, just as she had found the words to talk about the land development project, she found them to talk more about what happened with Grady. After she explained, she concluded with "I just feel so used. Like all Grady was trying to do was placate me enough with attention so that I wouldn't file a lawsuit for negligence against him."

"Did you even have anything but a bump after

hitting your head?"

"Not really." Danica brought her hand to the spot at her temple, the point of impact no longer visible. Still, today made it seem like she was branded with the hit she took. She even flashed to Owen. Now there was someone who had taken a real hit, someone with residual consequences that legitimately affected him long after the point of impact. Danica nursed a bruise, had a small headache, but that was it. "He completely misunderstood me in thinking I would do something like that." She could say those words to Paige, but she also admitted privately that she could have overreacted.

Paige held the line as if contemplating before she replied. "He's a new business owner. Still, you need to peel back the layers of this."

"What do you mean?"

"Was Grady the one concerned?"

"Yes."

"From what you said, wasn't it also Iris?"

"Her too."

"Who was more concerned?"

The answer to that question involved a mental replay of earlier. Danica did that, though it was difficult to separate initiated words.

"And if you don't know, give Grady the benefit of the doubt. At least consider talking to him about it."

That much Danica hadn't done. She let her backside do the talking as she walked away from a conversation she was scared to have.

"You can throw in the towel on this, just like you

could have thrown in the towel any time with the development project. Say your peace, cut your losses, and be done with it. Is that what you want?"

"No." Saying the answer felt as hallow as it sounded. As she talked through her last encounter with Grady, she took ownership of her over-the-top reaction. It wasn't even so much Iris herself as it was Danica's rustiness with a relationship. She should have taken a moment to pause before she acted. "I don't even know why I let it get to me."

"Then don't accept that." Paige's tough-love pep talk was exactly what Danica needed to hear. "You didn't quit with Cinnamon Ridge, and you don't have to quit with Dr. McHottie."

The sound of that nickname caused Danica to release a chuckle that she didn't know was in her chest. "That name," she censured.

"You know you like it."

Danica hadn't used it. But she had heard it semi-frequently from Paige, enough that every time she did, it made her smile.

Because Grady Urban was hot.

Yet that wasn't his only positive quality.

She had witnessed firsthand far more from him. He was thoughtful and spontaneous. Caring and generous. He was good with children and selfless with his time in volunteering at the school. Those actions were hard to forget.

The words of Danica's wizened friend were true. Her fingers grazed the edge of her turquoise glasses. "I'm not ready to lose my eye doctor."

Paige, like any good friend, read between the lines. "Then there's your answer."

~*~

Grady twisted the cap on a small bottle of eye drops. "One drop twice a day per eye," he instructed to the elderly patient who sat in the examination chair across from him.

The man had written the first name "Junebug" on his medical chart. Iris questioned whether that was his given name, to which he replied matter-of-factly, "No. That's what people call me." She then had asked what his name was, and he just repeated "Junebug."

Iris held the clipboard at an angle that only Grady could see, pointing to the statement "cash pay" noted next to the line for method of payment. Grady understood that since they weren't dealing with insurance paperwork, this patient could call himself whatever he wanted.

And Junebug was as much of a character as his name implied.

"How old are you?" Grady inquired after asking a few other questions and performing his work in the medical examination. The man's skin looked as old as the age indicated on his chart.

"Ninety-six years young." Junebug could have been Grady's grandfather or, even mathematically possible, his great grandfather. He looked in top shape for a man nearly a century old, and Grady told him so.

"Well, you know that they always say. The oldest

bananas make the sweetest bread." Junebug quipped.

Grady was getting used to the banter of local folks, but quirky comments like this still caught him off guard at times. He swallowed his unease. "I don't know anybody who says that."

Junebug shrugged. "Well, now you do."

Grady cleared his throat to stifle a laugh—or a cringe. He wasn't quite sure. "You seem to get around just fine. Any secrets to your longevity?"

"I do all right. I'm like a pecan: hearty and dependable. I eat plenty of those, too, so maybe that's the key to living a long life."

"Pecans?"

"Why not?" Junebug offered.

Grady untied his tongue enough to handle the reason Junebug called on the services of Spectacle Optique. "Let's talk about your eyes." Grady reviewed his diagnosis and then held up the bottle in his hands. "This will increase your tear production."

"Why do you want me cryin', Doc?" Junebug sized him up with skepticism.

"Not crying," Grady corrected his misunderstanding, knowing that having a man of this age change a daily routine was going to be a hard sell. "We're taking care of those dry eyes."

"It's 'bout time somebody stopped this itchin'. Will the drops do that?" Junebug's words were more of a challenge than a question.

"That's the idea."

"The idea?" Junebug pinned the doctor down for a better answer. "Or is this going to solve the problem?"

Grady should have seen this coming. After all, Junebug was being seen for an issue with his eyes. There didn't seem to be a question about the effectiveness of his hearing. "This will solve the problem." He screwed the cap back on to show Junebug how it was done before placing the bottle into his hands.

"Like you're givin' me gold." Junebug winked.

"Let's hope it works like a treasure."

"Good one, Doc." Junebug slapped his knee before grabbing the bottle. "You're not so bad, you know that?"

"Did someone say I was?"

"People," Junebug offered, as if beyond these few words, he didn't have a care in the world. "You know how they talk."

No, he actually didn't. That was part of the frustration with being new to the area and working so hard to develop a client base. But rather than pry personal information from a clam-shell mouth of an old man, Grady let that be the end of it. "Do you have any other questions for me?"

"Just one."

Grady readied himself for another senior-citizen complaint. He was receiving plenty of those regarding high costs, frustrating paperwork, and too many prescriptions. "What's your question?"

"Why is a sharp whippersnapper like you not hitched?" Junebug elbowed Grady and looked down at his ringless left hand. "Or do you just remove it at the office?" He winked and slid his gaze to Iris, as if she were somehow immune to hearing his insinuation.

She wasn't, and her exaggerated eye roll was her tell.

"I'm working on it with someone outside of the office" was the only response Grady could muster, and even that was a pretty pathetic answer given his love life.

"Well, keep working on it. My sweet ladybug is in heaven now, and I miss her every day. If you have the chance to find your lady, don't let her fly away."

Easier said than done, Grady wanted to say. But, instead, he offered a polite "Thank you" and helped Junebug from his seat. He steadied the old man before he took his time heading out the door, leaving Grady with thoughts about relationships.

Was a romantic relationship really this difficult— or was Grady just making it so? Like anything else, relationships took work. And maybe Grady was just taking the easy way out. After all, he fought to open Spectacle Optique. So when it came to matters of his heart, why was Grady unwilling to fight?

He wasn't. He passed the paintings which he loved and realized there were some desires worth pursuing.

Art.

Careers.

And Danica Lara.

TWENTY-ONE

The hallways of Seguin Elementary School buzzed with student excitement. "It's Friday," a teacher whom Danica only recognized by sight and not by name strode past her on the way to her Friday DEAR time with Owen. The kids all clutched library books and chatted with the excitement of their version of an out-of-classroom field trip. The teacher pivoted mid-stride to place a finger to her lips, but only the first few kids in line saw. Danica shrugged her best show of sympathy for the responsibilities the woman bore before making herself as invisible as possible when she ducked out of the way of the students.

Stepping inside Mrs. Livingston's classroom, she took off a casual blazer she had thrown over the shoulders of her sheath dress. As she folded the fabric across her arm, she looked up to see Grady staring.

Hard.

He stood as she walked toward the table that, from the first day, she had claimed as hers. "Good morning," she offered, keeping her language stiff and formal. Yet when her eyes met his, his gaze returned a sparkle that loosened the uncomfortable tightness inside of her chest.

"I'm glad to see you," he offered in return, pulling

out her chair.

It was a chivalrous move to make, though Danica didn't want to draw attention to the two of them anymore than perhaps had already been done by Grady's action. She gave a polite nod in gratitude and sat quickly. There were a few other mentors already in the room, but as was typical of the group, those who were nearest to one another paired up for polite chats before the children arrived.

And with no one on one side of her table, that left her with just Grady on the other.

Not like it was mandatory to have a conversation before the kids arrived.

Still, as Danica turned to hang her lightweight blazer over the back of her chair and stow her purse next to the inside of the table's legs, she knew she could only force little motions for so long before she would look fidgety. And looking fidgety when she was nervous anyway to be around Grady wasn't a look she cared to wear.

He sat after she did, the shadowing of her motions a familiar tug toward previous closeness they had shared. As he moved, Danica couldn't help but notice Grady's perfectly pressed shirt, the way the top button hung open in a crisp V-shape that accented his neck and teased the slightest portion of skin from a chest that she knew more intimately when her body was pressed against it during the kisses they shared.

She caught herself daydreaming, and she pushed the corner of her glasses and cleared her throat. Stick with prim thoughts, Danica.

But even an interior pep talk wasn't enough to stop her from reacting to sensations she didn't even know she had captured from Dr. Grady Urban.

That scent. Whatever cologne he wore mingled with that clean, antiseptic smell that was characteristically medical, an aroma that reignited her memories of enjoyable encounters shared week to week since their first introduction.

Still, there was more.

That skin. Grady's alabaster skin stood out among most others in the room, whose limbs and faces had been bronzed by summer sun. He glowed, but in an entirely different way.

Those eyes. Danica couldn't help but sneak a glimpse, and behind his hipster frames, his bright blue ones dazzled.

Human attraction could be a real beast.

Danica crossed her legs, angling her kitten heel away from Grady. She swung her foot in a nervous pattern, hoping to find an outlet for releasing thoughts she couldn't control. Why did such magnetism always sucker-punch her at the most inopportune times?

She sensed Grady leaning toward her, perhaps about to say something, but all that reached her ears instead was a ringing "Good morning!" greeting from Mrs. Livingston as she rounded the corner into the room. She clasped her hands upon seeing how many adults had already arrived, singing their praises with a string of compliments to grab everyone's attention and solicit smiles.

Then she hit the volunteers with a request.

"I want to do something special for the kids to celebrate autumn." She motioned for everyone to come closer, as if leaning across the tables at which everyone sat would result in some kind of football huddle. Danica uncrossed her legs enough to oblige, placing her elbows on the edge of the smooth surface. She tried to focus on Mrs. Livingston, not at all toward Grady as he made a motion toward the same.

Having everyone's attention, Mrs. Livingston went further into her idea. "The kids are making marvelous progress, and I'd like to treat them to a little celebration. Something low key but still celebrating reading."

"Like a fall festival in the classroom?" One of the volunteers piped up from the back of the room.

"Yes, like that. Only it has to be during our designated forty minutes."

Others started chiming in with their ideas and questions. Typically associated with a school fall festival were carnival type games, face painting, craft booths, fun food. But Mrs. Livingston envisioned a twist on that. "All books!"

Light bulbs seemed to click to life above the heads in the room one by one.

"How about classroom games about books?"

"Like a spinning wheel or memory cards."

"We can have musical chairs to lines from an audio book!"

"For book prizes!"

Ideas were being fired faster than a surprise story ending, and Mrs. Livingston was eating it up.

"Wonderful! All of these ideas are simply wonderful!" She clasped her hands in glee that she could count on her volunteers to be on board.

"I can probably get the university to donate some goodie bags," one member of the admissions staff from the local private institution offered.

"We've got pens and pencils for giveaways," a teller from a downtown bank added.

"I'll check with the public library to see if they have any titles they're taking out of circulation that they might want to unload." A woman raised her hand as she spoke to signal her willingness.

"And I can start a book drive at the office." Grady's voice was a pleasant shock of familiarity and sound. "Maybe get some of the clients to donate books that we can give away to the kids." It was the first time he spoke aside from their clipped arrival exchange, and hearing him in normal conversation was oddly settling for Danica.

"Such generous offers all around!" Mrs. Livingston's grin now appeared to be permanent on her face. "And, Dr. Urban, you are an angel in this community for what you are doing for the kids. It's such a delight to have a business owner among us." She motioned to the clock on the wall, which signaled there were but a couple of minutes to go before the official start of DEAR time. "The kids will be here any minute. Now, to head up this Fall Book Fest, we'll need some leadership. Dr. Urban, can I count on you for that?"

Grady nodded. "Yes ma'am."

"And as a co-chair for this, how about…" Mrs. Livingston looked directly to the one person sitting closest to Grady. "You, Danica?"

She really didn't leave her with much of a choice.

Danica cleared her throat, swallowed her surprise, and responded with a curt "sure" in reaction to practically being volun-told to do this.

She was now being forced to spend time with Grady Urban as co-chairs of the Fall Book Fest. It wasn't anything like a Barry Van Soyt partnership, but it was still as sudden as their agreement with Cinnamon Ridge had been.

If she stayed focused on developing this reward for the kids, it would be smooth sailing. But that was only if she could keep personal developments at bay.

And as Danica found herself staring a little too longingly at Grady's mouth, mentally replaying what had been shared with him in intimacy, she didn't trust herself enough to do that.

~*~

Grady really didn't need another project for which to be responsible.

But Mrs. Livingston had carved a special place in his heart for this program, and Alexis herself had done the same. The girl's toothless grin, her hard work, and her impressive weekly improvement were enough to quiet Grady when it came to any objection to helping with a project that would benefit these children.

When he agreed to Mrs. Livingston's outreach, he

hadn't expected Danica to be placed alongside him for the project. But he was secretly grateful that was the case.

He might just have to thank Mrs. Livingston with an apple next week. She couldn't have known the favor this was doing him—or did she?

As Mrs. Livingston turned to greet the line of children at the door, Grady swore she winked his direction.

He blinked back the image, unsure if his eyes were playing tricks, if he was reading too much into innocuous actions, or if his own emotions were finally having their say.

Whatever the case, he had to slide his analysis aside to focus on the ear-to-ear grinning third grader bopping his way. "Don't you look happy today?"

Alexis took the seat next to him, laying two books she carried atop the table as if they bore the weight of anvils.

"Those are big books."

"From the school library," she replied, her voice a perpetual whisper. It was as if everything she said held secret power. And as she showed the books to Grady, that might as well have been true. "This one's got a dragon. He breathes fire and picks flowers." She pointed to the picture on the front. "And this one," she restacked the books and showcased the second, "is about a pirate cat that can talk."

"A pirate cat?" Grady pointed to the cartoon drawing of an eye patch strapped across a whiskered feline's head. Only one of its cat eyes was visible. "I don't believe I've ever heard a story of a pirate cat."

"I'll read it to you." Alexis opened the cover, unlocking a story which she read with pristine pronunciation and careful consideration. She paused at the end of every sentence. She giggled with delight at the humorous pictures. She even gave a raspy "Argh, walk the plank" when it was time.

Grady had to help her with the word scallywag, but beyond that, this girl had it all together. "Great job, Alexis!" Grady cheered her skills at the end of the book, and their time continued to pass smoothly. They also had some comprehension questions to work through on a worksheet, and Alexis tackled that with enthusiasm when it was time.

Their forty minutes passed with lightning speed.

"Oh, rats. It's over already?" Alexis mumbled what Grady was thinking.

As Grady looked at her face, he saw a child who had come alive during the last few weeks thanks to this program. That was the reason he was willing to say yes to an additional time commitment with the planning of the Fall Book Fest.

Time with Danica was just a nice bonus.

The kids were called to the front of the room. "Line up, little ones." Mrs. Livingston herded everyone back, shepherding them like lambs out the door as they waved good-byes to their mentors. As Danica grabbed her blazer to swing around her shoulders and reached for her purse, Grady made his own move. "Care to get together to talk about the Book Fest? We could start planning next week."

"That would be fine." Danica steadied the straps of her purse over her shoulder.

"Don't worry. I know your work schedule. I won't impose."

"I wouldn't think it was in your nature to do that." Danica extended a slight smile.

That was enough of a message for Grady, who jumped at the opportunity and let his heart lead him into the right thing to say. "Over dinner. My place. Tuesday night."

Danica's face externalized the surprise Grady felt. Neither seemed to know from where the words came, but once they were out, there was no turning back.

For Danica.

For Grady.

"Dinner?"

"We'll plan. Don't worry about that."

Danica nodded.

But Grady couldn't gloss over the reality of why he said what he did. He needed to articulate the truth. "Consider it a date, Danica. I want to start over. Will you give me a chance to explain?"

Danica reached for the straps of her purse, hoisting it higher and shifting her balance from one foot to the other.

Grady held his breath. This was him on full display, honest and sincere. He had no time to rehearse lines, no time to woo Danica with a fancy memorized speech. This was simply a man standing in front of a woman vulnerable to a fault as he waited.

Danica tilted her head, and her eye contact with

Grady captured his attention as much as her softhearted, one-word answer. "Yes."

Some things in life were certainly worth the wait.

Grady beamed with inner joy that he hoped was showing externally.

"Only if you'll give me another chance too. I need to properly apologize for an overreaction of a misunderstanding." She looked around.

This wasn't the place to have such a conversation.

But the privacy of a residential space was.

"Say no more." Grady didn't want to lose this opportunity to get Danica alone, so he made them both focus on Tuesday as he gave his home address. "How does seven o'clock sound?"

"Sounds good," Danica agreed. "And I know where that street is," she said of his residence.

"Of course." With Danica's job, street names and house numbers were probably as ordinary to her as were the numbers with which Grady dealt in regard to eye care. "Don't bring a thing but yourself. This is my treat."

"Let's hope it is." Danica's teasing left Grady with hope as she stepped forward to head back to her office. He wanted to follow her to her car, spend just a bit more time with her, but easing back into interactions seemed best. He didn't want to overstep boundaries or rock the momentum that was developing.

TWENTY-TWO

Danica changed outfits three times on Tuesday evening.

"Why is it so hard to pick something to wear?" she mumbled to herself as she held up a peasant top in the full-length mirror, modeling it against her jeans. It was one of those pieces that was cute when it wanted to be.

But today wasn't the day for it.

"Urgh." She threw the top on the bed with the rest of the discarded shirts and rummaged further through her clothes, much more adept at picking out work clothes than casual clothes for an evening dinner with a member of the opposite sex. She wanted to look attractive without trying too hard—even though she was trying very, very hard.

Finally, Danica settled on her best pair of tight-fitting jeans, but she was still searching for the right top.

A cowl-neck blouse didn't look right.

Her favorite stretchy top with the tight floral pattern seemed a bit much.

She reached for a simple, button-down black shirt, brushed a wrinkle away with her hand, and held it at arm's length, considering it. The color was right for a funeral, not a Tuesday night dinner. The option met its throwaway fate too.

And what, exactly, was this dinner supposed to represent? Danica had her suspicions, but that wasn't enough to make her say no to Grady Urban. On the contrary, it was a pull toward his offer to explain his side of the guarded business story that put her squarely in the position to give him the benefit of the doubt.

Now if she could just find an outfit to wear for the occasion.

"The next shirt I touch is going to be it. No question." She held up her hand and spoke as if making an oath with her wardrobe. It gave an answer when Danica closed her eyes, placed her outstretched hand on the edge of a random hanger, and yanked.

Oh dear.

The shirt she held in her hands was good news and bad news. The good news was that it was a super soft cotton fabric. So comfortable! Its chocolate brown color brought out the deep tones of her eyes.

But the bad news?

It was a vintage t-shirt with a cartoon image.

What would Grady think of that?

A symbol of her childhood favorite cartoon featuring superhero cats graced the front. It wasn't a work shirt, but it was certainly appropriate for play. It had enough of a feminine cut that it was also fashion-forward in an unapologetically pop culture way.

She'd make it work.

She pulled the shirt over her head and shimmied it into place before adding a spritz of hairspray to lift her roots and revive them from a tired workday. She touched up her makeup, added a single chunky cocktail ring, and then put her glasses back into place before stepping back to judge her reflection in the mirror. She turned one way and then the other, trying to see herself as Grady would see her. But she really wouldn't know how he would view her until they came face to face.

He had called tonight a date, but was that fast talking? Was this really just Book Fest planning? Would there be a relationship apology? Or something totally different?

Danica didn't have the best track record for hypothesizing, so she stopped trying, grabbed her purse, and headed out the door to step into the possibility of some kind of future that involved Grady, at least minimally.

The address he gave wasn't far from downtown. Within Seguin, nothing really was, at least not until drivers passed the interstate. Seguin was one of the oldest towns in Texas, and part of its charm was in its layout, with older homes dotting wide residential streets that fanned from the town square. Danica always loved seeing these homes restored to their former glory. Restoration applications that she had seen recently did not disappoint.

Neither did Grady's.

His was a quaint yellow Victorian with gingerbread trim and a wraparound porch. Easy on the eyes from a distance, yet full of character up close.

A little like Grady himself. She smiled at the

realization.

Danica parked on the street, following the small sidewalk to the wooden steps of the house that was sandwiched in between other recently remodeled gems. So many long-standing homes had been renovated just like this one, their homeowners working to preserve the history of their investments for future generations.

This two-story structure didn't have the fresh veneer of its neighbors, but the potential was certainly there. It had solid bones but needed a little care to attend to peeling paint, a few missing spindles, and a weather-worn gable roof. Still, sturdy craftsmanship and impressive additions like beaded railing, stitch work at the eaves, and a front porch swing built for two were enough to make Danica want to grab a glass of lemonade and watch the sun go down from the glory of this spot.

Danica ascended the steps, her back to the sun as she brought her hand next to the screen door. She knocked her arrival in the absence of a doorbell.

Grady swung open the interior door and greeted Danica. "Hi there. Glad you made it." He edged open the screen door, stepping outside as he ushered her in front of him. "Come in. Come in."

Striking wood floors, tall ceilings, and intricate crown molding greeted her on the interior. "It's a bit of a work in progress," Grady apologized. "And a rental. The owner's got some renovations upstairs, and he's trying to figure out how to reroute some plumbing. Not much to look at right now." He closed the door behind them both. "But the downstairs turned out pretty well."

"I'll say." It wasn't fancy, but there was an understated elegance to the refinishing of what appeared to be original doors, window frames, and clapboard walls. Wainscoting ran the length of the hall into what looked like the kitchen at the far end.

"Living room," Grady gestured with one arm. "Sitting room" he gestured with the other. They made their way forward a few steps. "Bathroom through that door." They advanced again. "And we'll be eating here, in the kitchen."

Danica's eyes followed the light. "For a rental, this looks pretty settled."

Grady had accented the space with a couple of antique-washed wool floor rugs and clean-lined furniture that was neither stuffy nor dated. Like the modern approach to his office, he had taken a similar—though slightly more minimalist—approach to furnishing this private space.

"I've tried to make it livable." He held out an open hand. "Want me to set down your purse?"

"Sure." She handed it to him.

"Nice logo," he remarked as he turned to place her belongings on the seat of a slim bench that adorned one wall of the hallway. It looked like it could have at one time been a church pew. As he spun around, he was still smiling.

"You recognize this symbol?"

"That was my favorite cartoon growing up. It used to come on every day at three thirty in the afternoons."

"I know!" Danica practically shrieked with shared passion. They bantered with a quick exchange of their favorite characters, a couple of quotes, and interspersed laughter.

She did adore the sound of Grady's laugh.

"Come in here." He brought her and their conversation into the kitchen, the two of them walking a step closer than before. "This rental has a kitchen that works out pretty well."

"Not bad." It wasn't anything fancy. While the yellow-doored oven looked like it may have been older than Grady, the rest was in good shape. Everything was clean, neat, and airy. A single window above the sink gave a view of the fenced backyard. "Rentals in Seguin can be so hard to find."

"Tell me about it. I'm glad to have that search behind me. Do you know it was easier to find commercial space than residential space?"

"I believe you." She crossed her arms over her chest, taking in the interior and continuing their small talk. "There are lots of homes for sale but not too many decent ones to rent." Danica surveyed with her eyes. "But this looks fantastic."

"There's more that can be done. But it's working out."

"Are you helping with any of the remodel?"

"Me?" Grady raised an eyebrow, its arch just visible above the frame of his glasses. "I have no skills in that department. I can envision something, but I'll leave it to people with far more know-how than me to carry it out."

"A man who knows his limits," Danica chided.

Grady brought two fingers to his temple and rubbed. "I guess I walked right into that one."

They both exchanged a smile, and Danica was thankful that their ease of communication seemed to still exist. "Short term rental?"

"I've got it for a year. It was a great deal because the homeowner needed some income but wanted the freedom to continue to do the work himself. Good setup for us both. I'm not around much during the week, and all of my money has gone toward Spectacle Optique anyway."

But just as quickly as Danica felt at ease, she tensed slightly at the mention of his business and the turn of the conversation toward money.

"Why don't we sit?" Grady motioned to a small table with two chairs, half kitchen island and half intimate dining set. He pulled out a chair as Danica eased onto it. "Would you care for something to drink?"

"Sure." Danica's mouth seemed to remember the bitterness with which they had last ended things at the optometry office. She gladly accepted a glass of ice water from Grady, taking a sip to wash away the residual taste that had returned with the memory. Tonight needed to be a fresh start.

"And I have a bottle of wine in the fridge that I can uncork. Or if you're not up for that, I have a pitcher of sweet tea if you want that instead."

Options.

Choices.

She couldn't take back what had already transpired, but she could communicate. "I do want to talk about last week."

"I'm glad." Grady leaned forward, his eyes pleading for continued attention. "I want to talk about it too."

"I overreacted. I didn't wait for all the facts, and I jumped to a conclusion."

Grady didn't waste time in adding his own words. "I completely understand." He shifted in his seat so that his direct attention was to Danica's line of sight. No hiding, no averted gazes. "There was a big misunderstanding last week, and I didn't act fast enough to correct it. I want to correct it now."

"Me too." Danica was glad they were on the same page. "I'm sorry."

Grady's shoulders seemed to soften with those words as much as her own. "I am too." Then he addressed the source that had started all of this. "Iris was wrong. She had no right saying what she did."

Indeed, her words had stung. But stepping back from them, Danica would now see them for what they really were: immature and petty.

"I did not get involved with you out of sympathy or fear," Grady underscored. "I wasn't doing it because I felt sorry after you hit your head, and I didn't do it because I was worried you might bring a lawsuit against the business." He repeated, imploring her to understand, "I didn't get involved just to placate you."

The directness of his words was a fresh change of pace from what Danica previously thought, especially in regard to what her past experience had been with having tough conversations with men. Those encounters always seemed forced and stressful. Usually, she knitted together the bulk of the talk, enough to repair whatever damage had been done in a relationship so that it could at least move forward, bound by that bandage fix.

"I didn't come to Seguin to get involved with anyone, and I wasn't looking for a relationship when you walked into the office. I was looking to help a client."

Danica opened her eyes wide, testing the width of the turquoise glasses she loved. "And you did."

Grady smiled. "But then I grew to know you. Not as a client." Each word was measured, an earnestness in his tone that communicated his sincerity. "I got to know you as a person."

Grady grabbed her hand. The surprise of his touch snatched Danica's voice from a reaction, so she let her fingers do the talking. She intertwined hers with his, a consensual give and take of warmth and touch exchanged between them.

"I never expected to see you at the elementary school, but when I did, I couldn't stop seeing you there. There was a pull I didn't expect."

Danica knew what he meant. "I know." Yet she didn't want to dive too deeply into words she could regret, so she held her tongue while Grady continued.

"I saw your kindness, your selflessness. I saw your heart with those kids."

Danica couldn't help but think about Owen, a

turnaround kid who didn't have it all figured out yet but whom she was proud to say was on the right track.

"You are witty and enjoyable. You light up a room and you light up my world every time I see you."

Danica's cheeks warmed at the heavy compliments. Yet Grady didn't stop. And the details with which he spoke next about their fun in San Antonio made Danica understand that his words—this dinner invitation—was not for show.

It was arranged with heart and spoken from that selfsame place.

He squeezed her hand. "Danica, you are gorgeous inside and out. I'm a fool to have let you think that my intentions were anywhere else but on you. For that, I am sorry." Grady's words of apology tumbled into her ears, replacing the words she had previously heard Iris say. "Iris has a jealous personality. She's young. She thought that by insinuating things, she could wedge herself between a relationship." Grady quickly added, "which she did."

Thinking of how she had stormed off from Grady, Danica had to admit that the girl was successful.

"She may have gotten what she wanted then…" Grady's voice trailed as he brought a hand under her chin, gently lifting it so they were close. "But I didn't. I want something else now."

Danica's pulse quickened, jolting her insides. It took every ounce of restraint she had not to melt at Grady's touch, though she was able to quietly ask, "What is it that you want?"

"You." He leaned into Danica, closing the space

between them with a tender kiss. As Danica reciprocated, their shared passion erased all doubt of past intentions. Here, in the present, their lips exchanged what they had both held in their hearts.

Doubt and uncertainty were replaced by intimacy and understanding. And even though dinner was waiting for them, there was no rush. Besides, kissing was much more satisfying than anything Grady could have prepared.

TWENTY-THREE

Lemon chicken, green beans almandine, and poppy-seed-topped bread was now the trinity that comprised Danica's new favorite meal.

She would forever link those dishes with the night she and Grady rekindled a romance both of them were now ready to acknowledge. Past misunderstandings were behind them, and they had a future as bright as the stars in the big Texas sky that lit up in a nighttime show for them after they finished their meal and retired to the front porch swing. "This doesn't get nearly enough use." Grady wrapped his arm around the back of the swing, holding Danica as her body nestled against him.

She rested her head on his shoulder. "That is something I can help change." His body was warm, his scent comforting. Grady held her as he rocked the swing into gentle motion, a tight back and forth rhythm that generated a small breeze that fanned her hair. It lifted and lowered with each gentle movement they made together. "This feels nice."

Grady agreed as he placed a single, sweet kiss atop her forehead. Across their view, fireflies sparkled with their on-again/off-again light, creating patterns through the crisp evening air. Above the space where they flew, canopies of pecan trees created an atmosphere that made the residential spot feel much more secluded than it was. "This neighborhood has such great trees."

"Tell me about it."

The trees' blooms from spring had morphed into rich, leafy branches that drooped heavy with the upcoming fall harvest. Soon, pickers would be selling the area's highly-prized pecans from stands and entrepreneurial truck beds alongside the highways and at farmers' markets. Danica could practically taste their distinct flavor as she thought about all kinds of creative uses for the local product.

One of her favorites that helped usher in the season of fall was pecan-flavored coffee. She'd definitely have to get a few locally roasted bags to replace her current supply. But outside of the coffee shop, more devout foodies and experimental restaurateurs concocted all sorts of inventive uses, like mixing the oil into salad dressings or creating pecan-encrusted meats. Yet nothing could top her two favorite desserts of nutty pralines and pecan pie. She lightly licked her upper lip, the taste practically dripping from the trees around them.

"Did I tell you I saved a grove of pecan trees on some property at the edge of town?"

"Tell me about it," Grady insisted.

So Danica shared her project of Cinnamon Ridge, all the joys and pains and then the recent two-lot sale surprise.

Grady listened. And Danica was thankful to be in

the company of a man who did.

Only when she finished did he offer his congratulations along with praise for what she had accomplished.

"Thanks." Danica adjusted her body, wanting to stay close, "but I don't know if big projects like that are in my future after this one."

"Well, saving trees is something to be proud of." Grady bent his head toward her. "Speaking of old things, did I ever tell you about my elderly patient from last week?"

Danica winced at the awkward transition. "Don't you have a lot of those?"

"Point taken," Grady conceded. "So this patient of mine," he began, now speaking with heightened animation, "he just celebrated his ninety-sixth birthday, and I asked him about his secret to good health. Want to know what he said?"

"Surprise me."

"Pecans."

"That doesn't surprise me," Danica deadpanned,

Grady moved his upper body away. "It doesn't?"

"This is Seguin." She held out a hand, cutting through the space nearest to them as she looked out onto their scene. "Pecans, fresh air, opportunity. These are all good for people's health."

"I take it you're happy here?"

Danica settled back into Grady's embrace. "I'm happy here," she clarified, grabbing his hand in hers and letting their bodies find shared comfort again.

Grady resumed the rocking of the porch swing.

"So if you're done with land development projects, where does that put your availability for literacy projects?"

"You mean the Book Fest? I haven't forgotten." That was, after all, supposed to be the reason Grady invited Danica to his house in the first place.

But she knew better.

"Do you think we ought to talk about some plans for that?"

"We can." Danica squeezed Grady's hand, curling into him and letting her voice purr her availability. "I've got all night."

~*~

While Grady was as eager to extend their time together into the rest of the evening and talk about the Book Fest, there was still something more personal he longed to share with Danica.

"I want to tell you something." His voice was slow and his volume low as he kept her close.

"OK." She nuzzled against him, their breathing sharing a cadence.

Grady Urban inhaled deeply, his chest rising beneath Danica's head. It rose and fell with Grady's intake. But he couldn't quite speak.

"You're making me nervous." She brought her hand to his chest and held it flat against his heart. She tilted ever so slightly to meet his gaze. "Are you all right?"

Grady looked into her eyes, the reflection of his

own shining back to him even between their respective layers of lenses. This is my life, he couldn't help but think as he looked at her through the work he had done. Thanks to his optometry business, Grady was able to prescribe Danica the lenses she ultimately picked to fit inside those cute turquoise frames. He had helped her, and his office is where they had met. Never in a million years would he have guessed he would follow through on a romance with a patient.

Yet here they were.

Grady Urban was the town's newest optometrist. Yes, his life was one that included glasses, contacts, equipment, and diagnoses. Fitting others with vision assistance was his life.

But as he held Danica, he knew there was more than what he had seen. Or done.

There was her.

And whether he was too wrapped up in work or too preoccupied to see it before, he saw it now.

With certainty.

With absolution.

Holding her gaze, he saw more than he ever had. "Danica," he started slow and he found his voice again. "I want to share something with you. About how I see."

Danica adjusted her position, righting herself halfway at the shift in tone with Grady's words. "Is everything all right?"

He tucked a loose strand of her hair behind the frames of her glasses, the very ones for which he was responsible. It gave him pride to help another person see the world better.

But Danica had helped him see better. That's what he wanted to tell her. "Everything is fine." He settled the strand of hair lovingly behind her ear, letting his hand fall atop her shoulder and rest. "You see the world through your eyes, and I see it through mine." He felt his heart skip a beat inside his chest, the weight of what he was expressing suddenly real to him. "But since I've met you, I've seen the world through yours too. Being with you—whether at the office, in San Antonio, at the school, or just talking—has done that. And I've never had such an easy connection like this with another person."

Danica bit her lip.

"It's true." Grady hoped he wasn't sounding cliché. Because when it came to the strength of his feelings, they were genuine and real. "When I look at you, I see the world as it is made to be seen. Fresh and fair. Dazzling and full of delight." He was describing the atmosphere she created as much as he was describing her. "That's you," he said simply. "Sparkling."

Danica released her bottom lip as it joined her top one to slide into a smile.

Grady responded with one of his own. They shared companionable silence, a moment of bliss that was as magical as the far-reaching light from the twinkling stars above. He lowered his hand from Danica's shoulder, and her hand found his. Their fingers pretzeled into one another, a connection each to each that seemed to be custom-fitted.

Connections physical and emotional were higher than Grady had ever experienced them. "You are a woman I didn't even know I needed to see. But now that I do, I don't want to look away."

"Then don't." Danica leaned into him, her lips meeting his in a satiating connection that reflected her own inner emotion. Satisfying yet sweet, there was no reason to rush.

Or talk.

Their kisses did the communicating for them in connections that carried into an evening that was theirs alone.

~*~

Slices of warm pecan pie and mugs of steaming, nut-infused coffee became routine parts of the week for Danica and Grady as the calendar wound its way into fall. "Another great reason to love Seguin." Grady agreed with Danica. Both of these concoctions were home runs.

They hoped their Fall Book Fest with the DEAR kids would be as well.

Throughout the last month, three more kids had been added to the Friday class, and Danica and Grady were both instrumental in helping find mentors in the community for the additional children. They also worked with the other volunteers to plan an incredible Friday morning for all fifteen kids.

On the day of the event, Grady cleared his schedule completely, and Danica was able to finagle an extra half hour leave time from Cameron at the appraisal district. Setting up for the event was so much fun, with Grady and Danica both laughing as much as they expected the kiddos to do.

Each of the mentors was encouraged to dress in some type of literary-themed or storybook-inspired attire. Grady arrived in a red and white striped Cat-in-the-Hat hat, and Danica donned a scarlet cape and picnic basket. "You're the cutest Little Red Riding Hood I've ever seen," Grady whispered.

"Watch it, wolfy," Danica teased, swinging her picnic basket to keep him at bay.

"I'm a cat." Grady pointed to his hat. "Completely harmless."

"Save it for the weekend." Danica winked, and Grady's pale skin flushed with future possibility.

The two of them, however, weren't the most creative of the bunch. One volunteer made herself into a walking library card using a sandwich board approach. Another wore a popular sketch from a graphic novel series all the kids loved. Danica had been introduced to it by Owen, so she knew he would be thrilled when he saw this volunteer. He went around the room, practicing his quotations of a few lines from one of the books to different adults so he'd be ready for the kids when they arrived.

"The kids are going to go absolutely bananas." Mrs. Livingston was beyond delighted at the way everything was coming together.

And so was Danica.

Each child received a goodie bag with two books

based on their reading level, though they could play a bean bag toss game in one corner of the room for a chance to win more books. At the pumpkin decorating station, there were also fall-themed books from which each child could choose a title. Two more fun stations rounded out the other corners of the room. There, students could design their own book covers and have their pictures taken for "author biographies" that each child would be writing the following week for their next in-class DEAR time project.

Mrs. Livingston did give permission for snacks, so there were sugar cookies in the shape of books; cupcakes decorated to look like apples, each with a bookworm coming out of the top; and fruity punch that Danica hadn't yet labeled with a funny literary name.

Danica held a permanent marker over a blank piece of paper. "Maybe I'll just have the kids brainstorm a name."

"Good idea," Grady agreed. "They'll probably come up with all sorts of wacky ideas."

"Oooh!" Danica's eyes lit as she capped the marker. "We can make a contest! Best name gets an additional book!"

"There's a neat hardback copy of one I saw in the stack over there—"

"I'll get it!" Danica was off, her cape flapping wildly behind her as she strode toward her newest mission.

Mrs. Livingston clapped her hands for everyone's attention. "It's almost time." She thanked all of the volunteers for their work, and then she specifically called out Grady and Danica. "These two leading the charge helped bring order to this event, and we are so grateful." Applause followed her remarks, and both were gracious with receiving the acknowledgement. Still, as Danica gave a character-appropriate curtsy and Grady waved his hand and tipped his costume hat, they both knew they couldn't have done anything without the support of all the others in the room.

"Truly a team effort," Grady interjected.

More applause filled the space until Mrs. Livingston shushed the crowd with "It's time! It's time!"

The children entered like soldiers returned from duty, their happy faces beaming at the sight of the volunteers. This was their homecoming. Wide eyes of shock took in the games, the food, and the total transformation of the space. Looks of recognition registered one by one as the children guessed costumes and understood the jokes inherent with some of the labels, prizes, and food.

All throughout the Book Fest, literacy was celebrated. Smiles and compliments abound, and every child was made to feel special. The undercurrent of reading helped bring stories and their joy alive for students in ways that reached new heights today.

Alexis attached herself to Grady's leg in a bear hug a few times during the event, showing that toothless grin that spoke volumes about how much she was enjoying herself.

Owen wasn't one for affection, but he held his

head higher than Danica had seen and interacted incredibly well during his turn at various stations. When Danica came by the pumpkin decorating station to check on his creation, she asked if he was having a good time.

"This is fun." Those three words of affirmation were all Danica needed to hear. He pointed to a permanent marker line that he made near the top of the pumpkin's face he had drawn.

"What's that?" Danica pointed to the jagged sketch.

"A scar," he shrugged. "Mine's not so bad. So I figured the pumpkin could use one too."

"I think it adds character."

She didn't intend for her words to be a pun, but sharp-sensed Owen laughed at the witty use. "I get it. Character?"

Even Danica had to laugh at that.

She had fun as well, and near the end of their allotted time, she sidled up to Grady. They looked over the classroom, glee happening wall to wall. "Well, what do you think, Doc?"

He touched the corner of his glasses, squinting through the frames. "I see bright futures ahead for these little ones."

"And for the rest of us?"

Grady turned to Danica, lowering his glasses on his nose so he could look straight into her eyes, unencumbered by even transparent lenses. She mirrored the same, laughing as she did. To the kids, they must have looked as if they were playing a game with one another.

But with them, there was no game. It was simply Danica and Grady, looking into each other's eyes and seeing a reflected view that both were happy to share.

A Devotional Moment

"Give, and it will be given to you. A good measure, pressed down, shaken together, running over, will be put into your lap; for the measure you give will be the measure you get back." ~ *Luke 6:38*

We're instructed to be generous with one another. We know this, but sometimes we miss the mark, we hold a grudge or simply choose ourselves or our fear over giving to others. But, God knows that we are better, happier, more fulfilled people when we give, and so He tells us that by whatever measure our generosity flows, so will the joy we get back.

In **Seeing Us**, the protagonist has a giving spirit, but he's a little reluctant and unsure of whether he actually has what it takes to help. When he finally puts aside that fear and embraces the task of helping a child, he realizes a joy he didn't before know he could feel.

Have you ever been afraid to help? Perhaps you felt unprepared or that you lacked a necessary skill. Maybe you were hurt in the past when you tried to help, and that fear of being hurt again stops you from helping others. It's important to remember the generosity God has shown to you. From food, clothing, a job, a place to live, all the way to salvation and everything between. As he has shown you generosity, so you should be generous to others. Let the fear slide away. Being a child of God gives you all the credentials you need. In so doing, you'll discover an inner joy that can't be matched by any self-centered thought or deed.

LORD, HELP ME TO HAVE A GIVING SPIRIT. AS YOU HAVE FREELY GIVEN TO ME, LET ME BE ABLE TO GIVE TO OTHERS AND TO BE A LIGHT TO THE WORLD. IN JESUS' NAME I PRAY. AMEN.

Pecan Pie

AN ORIGINAL RECIPE FROM AUDREY WICK
AND PELICAN BOOK GROUP

In *Seeing Us*, Danica's mouth waters for pecan pie, and it's a dessert that she and Grady enjoy together as their relationship continues to grow. Seguin is the heart of Texas's pecan country, but if you've never made pecan pie, don't let the process frighten you. It's easy if you follow this recipe. The pie crust is a no-fail approach that can be used with all kinds of fillings, outside of just this pecan recipe. But if you are short on time, you can also substitute an unbaked store-bought crust.

Serves: 8
Prep Time: 10 minutes
Cook Time: 40 minutes
Cooling Time: 1 hour

CRUST
1 ½ cup flour
3 T. milk
1 T. sugar
½ cup vegetable oil

PIE FILLING
4 eggs
½ cup brown sugar
¾ cup corn syrup
1 tsp. vanilla extract

1 tsp. butter-flavored extract
1 T. melted butter
1 cup pecan halves

DIRECTIONS
Preheat oven to 450 degrees.

For the crust, mix all ingredients together in a bowl, then press the mixture into a 9-inch pie pan. Set aside.

In a bowl, beat eggs with mixer until frothy.
Fold in all remaining ingredients.
Pour into pie shell.
Bake for 10 minutes at 450 degrees.

Reduce oven temperature to 350 degrees and bake for an additional 30 minutes.
Cool.

Serve warm, if desired. Pie can then be kept in the refrigerator for several days.

Author Bio

Audrey Wick is a contemporary romance and women's fiction author who is also a full-time professor of English at Blinn College in Texas. She believes the secret to happiness includes life-long learning and good stories. But travel and coffee help. She has journeyed to over 20 countries—and sipped coffee at every one. Connect with her at audreywick.com and on Twitter and Instagram @WickWrites.

Thank you

We appreciate you reading this White Rose Publishing title. For other inspirational stories, please visit our on-line bookstore at www.pelicanbookgroup.com.

For questions or more information, contact us at customer@pelicanbookgroup.com.

White Rose Publishing
Where Faith is the Cornerstone of Love™
an imprint of Pelican Book Group
www.PelicanBookGroup.com

Connect with Us
www.facebook.com/Pelicanbookgroup
www.twitter.com/pelicanbookgrp

To receive news and specials, subscribe to our bulletin
http://pelink.us/bulletin

May God's glory shine through
this inspirational work of fiction.

AMDG

You Can Help!

At Pelican Book Group it is our mission to entertain readers with fiction that uplifts the Gospel. It is our privilege to spend time with you awhile as you read our stories.

We believe you can help us to bring Christ into the lives of people across the globe. And you don't have to open your wallet or even leave your house!

Here are 3 simple things you can do to help us bring illuminating fiction™ to people everywhere.

1) If you enjoyed this book, write a positive review. Post it at online retailers and websites where readers gather. And share your review with us at reviews@pelicanbookgroup.com (this does give us permission to reprint your review in whole or in part.)

2) If you enjoyed this book, recommend it to a friend in person, at a book club or on social media.

3) If you have suggestions on how we can improve or expand our selection, let us know. We value your opinion. Use the contact form on our web site or e-mail us at customer@pelicanbookgroup.com

God Can Help!

Are you in need? The Almighty can do great things for you. Holy is His Name! He has mercy in every generation. He can lift up the lowly and accomplish all things. Reach out today.

Do not fear: I am with you; do not be anxious: I am your God. I will strengthen you, I will help you, I will uphold you with my victorious right hand.
~Isaiah 41:10 (NAB)

We pray daily, and we especially pray for everyone connected to Pelican Book Group—that includes you! If you have a specific need, we welcome the opportunity to pray for you. Share your needs or praise reports at http://pelink.us/pray4us

Free eBook Offer

We're looking for booklovers like you to partner with us! Join our team of influencers today and periodically receive free eBooks!

For more information
Visit http://pelicanbookgroup.com/booklovers

How About Free Audiobooks?

We're looking for audiobook lovers, too! Partner with us as an audiobook lover and periodically receive free audiobooks!

For more information
Visit
http://pelicanbookgroup.com/booklovers/freeaudio.html

or e-mail
booklovers@pelicanbookgroup.com